Copyright © 2019 by Sabrina Rose

This book is a work of fiction. Names, characters, places, and incidents either are the product of the author's imagination or are used fictitiously and are not to be construed as real. Any resemblance to actual persons, living or dead, business establishments, events, or locales or, is entirely coincidental. No portion of this book may be used or reproduced in any manner whatsoever without writer permission except in the case of brief quotations embodied in critical articles and reviews.

Sabrina's Contact Info:
Instagram: Calirosee_
Email: Calirosee1221@gmail.com

Sophia

Summer 2014'

    Finally arriving at the house party some guys from around the way were throwing, I surveyed the crowd. I didn't want to go but Melody insisted that I needed to live a little before I went away to college. High School was over, and we officially graduated. Of course, leave it up to Melody to make me feel guilty if I didn't go along with her crazy summer antics before leaving to start college. I don't know about her, but I had enough of the Brooklyn air and needed an escape and if this was my only way out, then so be it. Another reason why she wanted to come to this party was to see her boo, Drew. Drew was a guy who went to our high school, well barely anymore. Their relationship was more on the down low because he knew her older brother, Black.

    "Yo what's good Sophia?" I heard someone call out. Looking around, I saw that It was Jah. All the guys were cool with me I guess because they saw me as one of them. We sat around, cracked jokes, things like that. No, I wasn't a dyke, but I wasn't a girly girl either. I just preferred different clothing from how girls usually would dress. Instead of wearing dresses and skirts, I always wore jeans, or maybe shorts on a good day. I wasn't into makeup or nails, but I wasn't into games or sports either, I was just me. I gave Jah and the rest of the guys a hug and we proceeded into the house. Weed smoke instantly smacked me right in the face.

"Look at my baby daddy," Melody whispered in my ear.

I turned my head to the direction she was gazing at and low and behold it was Drew. He saw her and blew her a kiss that made her blush like no tomorrow. *It would be nice to feel that way*, I thought. We walked over to where Drew was at and Melody gave him a hug and whispered something into his ear. Instead of a hug, I gave him and his friends a head nod.

"You here with your girlfriend I see," James said, laughing.

James was an asshole, He always brought up that me and Melody were girlfriends. *What part did people not understand? I don't like girls!* Just because my clothes weren't revealing, or I didn't care enough to make trips to the nail salon every two weeks didn't mean I was gay. I rolled my eyes at him slowly, making sure he caught my response.

"James, leave my best friend alone, you're not even her type! Nor are your pockets!" Melody said sticking up for me like she always did. James knew better than to talk smack back to her because everybody knew who her brother was and didn't want any of that heat coming to them.

"Sophia, I'm going to the bathroom I'll be back," Melody said. *I knew what that meant*, I thought. Whenever we got around Drew, they always disappeared quickly. I figured to go have sex or something. Sex must have felt real good the way they acted within five minutes of seeing one another. She was going to be grown with Drew's ass and wasn't coming back anytime soon. *This is why I didn't want to come in the first place!* I don't understand why they kept their relationship on the down low because wouldn't her brother feel better with her messing with somebody he personally knew instead of a stranger? Well that's how I saw it. Getting comfortable because I knew it was going to be a long night, I sat down on the couch. Jah came to sit next to me, rolling up. Good, at least I won't be lonely until Melody decided to come back.

Three hours later...

After a few shots and some weed, me and Melody was fucked up, literally.

"I called my brother to come and get us already. He's around the corner," she said.

"Okay" I replied.

"Bye Drew," she whispered giving him a hug before we walked away, sneaking in a kiss on his neck. Turning around to wave goodbye, his eyes were planted on her behind, that she made sure to add an extra switch to her walk. Just like she couldn't get enough of him, the feelings were mutual.

We are too old for this, I thought. Walking outside, her brother's shiny black Lexus was pulling up to the house.

"Hey brotherrrr," Melody said.

"Get your ass in the car!" He yelled. I got in the back with Melody. Black's friend Nino was sitting in the passenger seat. Sitting down, I let out a breath of relief. The AC was booming, and the seats were more comfortable than the cushion I was sitting down on for hours inside the house.

"Hey Black," I said.

"Your mother know you out here getting drunk with my sister?" he asked.

He always made it seem like he was so much older than us. Well, he was but it didn't seem that way. He's four years older than us at twenty-two. With me and Melody being eighteen, I don't think it's a problem with that. Black was cool though, and he never snitched on us. He just always told us to make sure we watched our surroundings and not get out of control and we were good. He always came when Melody called, which was dope as a sibling. Nobody couldn't deny the love he had for his little sister.

"Yup," I laughed.

"Umm Hmm, are going home?" He asked.

It was Friday and I really didn't want to be home, so I told him I was going with Melody to spend the night. Black was so fine! All the girls wanted him. People called him Black because he was very dark, and he just rocked with the name. He was Slim and had that fine coolie boy hair that fitted him perfectly. He always wore bright colors that went very nice with his skin, his beautiful skin. No tattoos or any marks, his skin was perfect. I give him props because he was fine but I see him as a brother, and I knew I could never get him so I never put that thought into my mind. I wouldn't want him either, between all the girls who fought over him, and all the attention he received from everybody, it would be too much to deal with.

"Girl he marked the shit up out of you neck," I told Melody. We were in her room now just talking about everything that happened tonight.

"I know right! He gets too excited," she laughed

"I see," I replied.

"We have the best quickies. It's always good though," she said looking in the mirror examining her hickeys smiling. Probably reminiscing about how they got there.

Recently I've been wondering what sex felt like. Yes, I was still a virgin, unfortunately... Not because I wanted to be one, but it just never happened. I'm not sweating it though. Getting up I went to use the bathroom before we laid down to go to bed. Walking from the bathroom I saw Black's door was left ajar. He had his own place but sometimes still crashed here at his mother's house, from time to time. Curiosity got the best of me as I walked towards his room. Looking inside I saw him lying on the bed with his phone in his hand, shirtless only with a pair of grey sweatpants on and you know what they say about those. His print was real! Yeah, I'm not experienced in that department but that doesn't mean I couldn't look or knew what is was. His room light was off but the light from the TV was good enough to get a clear view of him. He let out a small chuckle, taking a minute before he started to text on his phone as if he was thinking of a reply. Staring at him, my mind started to wonder about things I couldn't even understand. I wondered what someone sent him to make him laugh. I wondered if it was a female. Grabbing onto himself, he adjusted what was giving him that print that was easy on the eyes. That confirmed my suspicion that a female was whom he was talking to. His print seemed to start to grow bigger. Grabbing onto my chest, I felt a tingling sensation from my nipples. *That's weird, I don't think I ever felt that feeling before.* My mouth felt like it was watering. *What is going on right now?* I guess he felt me staring because he looked away from his phone and up at me.

"You need something?" He asked me. I stood there silent, not being able to use my words. He dropped his phone onto his chest, still staring. I wanted to say something but it's like my voice box suddenly was gone. *I think I needed something. Did I?*

"Uhm," I started to say. Something took over my body as I started to open his room door more. *What am I doing right now?* I thought to myself.

"Sophia!" I heard Melody scream my name.

"I like your car," I stupidly said. *Why the hell would I say that? I been in his car multiple times.*

Black looked at me so confused, shaking his head. Jumping back into reality I rushed to Melody room before he could even respond. "What happened?" She asked looking at me suspiciously. "Nothing I just tripped," I told her laughing it off.

Why would I say that stupid shit? I thought.

The Next Day...

"Okay Black I'm ready!" Melody called out. He was getting ready to drop her off at the movies. She wanted me to come too, but I already played the third wheel last night, so I wasn't playing it today. I would rather stay in the comfort of my bed. I stayed over at Melody's house a lot, so I had a pair of changing clothes I put on after I showered. Just some sweatpants and a t-shirt, nothing major. Looking in the mirror, I ran my fingers through my light brown hair. My roots were sweated out due to the humidity and not wrapping my hair last night. Me and Melody talked and joked until the wee hours of the morning, dozing off.

"Girl look at my hair! Do you have a hat?" I asked Melody.

"Me? In a hat? You know you would never see that. Let me ask my brother-" she suggested walking towards her room door.

"No," I cut her off, grabbing her arm before she can even finish.

"Why not? You know he won't say no to me," she said walking out of the room.

A few minutes later she returned with a New York Yankees fitted. "Dang, that's all he had available?" I asked.

"Same thing I said, he told me, beggars can't be choosers. You better stop playing and rep your city girl!" she jokes.

"Fine..." I mumbled putting the oversized fitted on.

"Aright, come on! I got some shit to handle today," Black said standing outside of Melody door. "Nice hat," he smiled at me.

"Oh, why thank you," I responded sarcastically.

"It's one of my favorite hats," he said making me smile before grabbing the front of the hat, pulling it down.

"Leave her alone, jerk!" Melody laughed.

"Shut up before your ass be walking," He said as we walked out the door.

*****

Finally, we were on our way to drop me off home after sitting in the movie theaters parking lot for about ten minutes. Black was concerned about why I wasn't attending. He kept pressing if it was because of money, if so, he got me. It was far from that, but he was so damn consistent, I had to practically beg him to pull off. The real reason of course being that I didn't want to be the third wheel and really didn't want to be around Drew's friends. After finally taking my word, he started the car and we were on our way.

"Speak," Black said into his phone.

"*Speak*? What do you mean speak? That's not how you answer the phone!" A girl voice came booming through the car phone. *I wonder if that's the girl he was texting last night.*

"Do you pay my phone bill?" He asked the caller.

"No… but…" the loud chick over the phone said, suddenly lowering her voice down.

"Exactly. Now what do you want because you are ruining my mood?" Black asked.

"Well…umm… remember when you said you were going to pay for my hair to get done… Well, did you change your mind?" The called asked.

"Man, how much is it?" Black asked.

"I'm only getting braids so just two hundred and fifty dollars the most," she said.

"Yeah aright. I'm going to be in front of your door in about five minutes, hurry up because I don't have all day," he said ending the call.

"Girlfriend problems?" I asked laughing.

"Hell no," he said making a U turn.

"Sure does seem like it, making U turns and shit," I said.

"Oh, I see you got jokes. Nah Sophia, she isn't my girl. More like a, homegirl," he responded.

"*Homegirl*?" I repeated.

"Yeah, homegirl. When I need her to do something for me no matter what time of day it is or whatever it is, she comes through so sometimes I look out for her. I got a few homegirls," he said laughing.

"Do you have sex with these *homegirls*?" I asked emphasizing on homegirl.

"Now you are asking too many questions little girl," he said laughing.

"Little? You do know I'm eighteen, right?" I asked.

"Oh, my fault, I forgot you grown," he said pulling up to a brownstone building. A brown skinned chick came running down the stairs. Her body looked like the famous girls on Instagram. She had on a red crop top with some black biker shorts. Her hair was in the finger waves style. *Didn't she say she was getting braids? I know she better be going to the Africans because they would be the only hope she has to catch that*, I laughed to myself.

"Hey baby," she said, leaning over into his car trying to kiss him. Noticing what she was doing, he moved his head.

"You know we don't do that," he said laughing. Embarrassment showed all over her face.

"Yeah okay," she said now leaning up with her hand on her hips. Her biker shorts were so tight, you can see the print of her vagina. Digging in his pockets, Black pulled out three one hundred-dollar bills and passed it to her.

"Thanks daddy," she said as I busted out laughing. I never saw a female call a guy daddy before, of course that wasn't their father.

Noticing me in the back seat she finally spoke, "Oh, I didn't know you hang out with little dykes," she said laughing. I immediately started to feel uncomfortable. Here I was in oversized cap and sweatpants. She was a full-figured beautiful woman and I was still petite with barely any breast and hips.

"I'm not a dyke," I spoke up rolling my eyes.

"Right," she said laughing.

"Karma, what you need to be doing is going to get your ass fixed instead of trying to clown somebody. Your left ass cheek is hanging!" He said laughing, starting the car.

"Fuck you Black!" She yelled, holding onto her butt.

"Ain't worth it ma!" He said laughing pulling off.

Pulling up to my building ten minutes later, I thanked him and pulled on the door handle, trying to open the door.

"Can you unlock the door?" I asked him with an attitude, noticing he had the child safety lock on.

"What's wrong with you?" He asked.

"Nothing, nothing at all," I told him still pulling on the door handle.

"It's what Karma said?" He asked. *Oh, that's her name,* I thought rolling my eyes.

"Karma and everybody damn else!" I finally let out.

"First and foremost, don't ever let no woman with a fake ass body say something that will get to you. It's obvious they were going through more insecurities than you. Two, yeah, I noticed you don't dress how my sister dress and all these other females and that's fine. Once you start dating and shit, if you can get a man without him noticing your body first, you already won. Never forget that," he said unlocking the door.

"How do you know I don't date?" I asked him with an attitude.

"Well do you?" He asked.

"Thanks Black, I appreciate it," I said getting out of the car, ignoring his question. Once I got to my front door, Black beeped his horn and I waved goodbye.

Black

"So, this job should be the last one for a minute," I spoke up. I was into a little of everything. My main source was this right here. I had a group of females that would rob niggas for me. Not hurting them physically or any shit like that, just slip a little something into their drinks and get as much cash as they can. Also, breaking into their ATM cards. The way I saw it, they should've never been slipping anyway to get played. You'll be surprised that most of the men are married anyway. I used to be slanging dope, the typical shit, but that was getting tiring. I didn't have time to be beefing with hating ass niggas, complaining about blocks and who made the most money. A young nigga like me was just trying to get paid! Feel me?

"Yes, I'm ready to get this over with," Karma said rolling her eyes. She was still mad about the other day on her childish shit. This was the first time I had her get into this shit, now she had me rethinking my decision.

"You can leave if you want to," I told her.

"Yeah because we don't need no negative energy around," Shay said. Me and Shay go way back, and she was down from when I first started this shit. People thought we fucked around, but nah it wasn't anything like that. I showed loyalty to the people that showed it to me, and Shay was definitely loyal. Karma kept her mouth closed because she knew Shay wasn't the one to play with.

"So, silence means everything is good?" Shay asked looking directly at Karma.

"Yeah..." she mumbled.

"Good, so here is the plan. Tonight, is the night! Randy thinks it's going to the best night of his life. Little does he know it's not. We been planning this for a month so it should be no fuck ups. His wife is out of town, so this is our night! If you want the money you deserve, like I said, it won't be any fuck ups. Please don't do anything stupid," Shay told Karma and Christina. Christina has been around for some time with her and Shay being close friends, so Shay thought it was best for Christina to do this one with her.

"So, you weren't going to respond to my text?" Karma asked me after sitting down next to me.

"I didn't see it," I lied.

"Why are acting that way towards me?" she asked.

"Girl, if your dick whipped ass won't stop nagging that man and get into GO mode! Damn, he isn't offering shit but a good time in bed to you, if that, and you over there crying and shit. Once you get your own damn money, a hard dick isn't going to mean shit to you! Damn, I hate yawl young girls!" Shay said going off. *Damn I wonder who broke her heart*, I thought.

"Don't pay her no mind," Christina said to Karma laughing.

We were in a Motel close by getting everything together. After this lick, I knew I would have enough put up, this shit was kind of getting old, but the fast money always pulled me back in.

Karma

  We finally arrived at the Loft Downtown, Brooklyn. I was a little nervous, of course with this being my first job. The girls reassured me that everything was going to be fine. Shay been talking to the guy Randy for a while, via the phone. His wife was out of town on a business trip, so he told Shay it was okay for her to come over. What he didn't know was that me and Christina was joining in on the festivities. All three of us had on black trench coats with black pumps. Under each of our trench coats, our bodies were decorated in lingerie. The color of my lingerie was red along with Christina. Shay's lingerie was white, standing out as the ringleader.

  Getting out the unmarked car, we held our heads down as we approached the building. Shay entered the code Randy gave her and granted us entry. Opening the door, we walked into a comfy loft. You could tell that a woman lives here just by looking at the décor. Suddenly, Randy appeared from a room in the loft with a bottle of Champagne and two glasses. I knew it was him from the pictures Shay showed us. "Hey… oh, I didn't know you were bringing company," Randy said shocked from seeing me and Christina.

"I'm just trying to make it a night that you will remember," Shay said walking over to Randy taking the glasses and bottle out of his hand, placing it on a table nearby. Walking back over to him, she grabbed his hand, directing him to sit on the couch. "You don't have anything stronger than this?" She asked Randy.

"Yeah, it's a mini bar in the kitchen area," he responded.

Nodding her head towards the kitchen, Christina took note and made her way over there. They were such pros; I didn't know the next move to take so I just took a seat next to Randy. Loosening his tie, Shay took it off of him and placed it in his lap making sure to grab onto his penis also. Letting it loose, she rubbed up and down on it through his slacks. Little beads of sweat started to form on the top of Randy's head. "So how long is your wife going to be out of town?" Shay asked him.

Clearing his throat, he answered, "Just for one night."

"Oh, so that means we have to hurry and make it worth it right?" Shay teased.

"So you are a dark kind of man?" Christina asked Randy walking to the area we were in with a bottle of Jack Daniels.

"Preferably, I guess," Randy said.

"Why do you seem so nervous?" Christina asked as she sat on his lap. Taking a glass, she poured a shot. Putting it to her lips and drank some of the alcohol, then telling him to drink the rest. Shay grabbed his face, so he can give her his undivided attention. Untying the black belt on her jacket, she opened it showing Randy what she had on underneath. His eyes opened up wider surprised. Looking from me to Christina, he realized we must of had the same thing on underneath also.

"I think he likes what he sees," Christina laughed getting up.

"Well do you?" Shay pressed.

"Well... Umm... Yeah..." he responded running his hands through his sandy brown hair. His cheeks were flushed with redness. Grabbing the bottle of Whiskey, he poured himself another shot.

"Where's the music?" I asked finally breaking my silence. Randy leaned up and picked up the remote off the table. Turning on the radio, Shay requested the station he should put on. At this point, I didn't know who was more nervous, me or Randy.

"Okay, time to get this party started," Christina said loosening her jacket. Following her lead, I loosened mine also.

*****

Inside the bathroom, I was looking in the mirror fixing the style of my braids. The alcohol hit Randy hard, but the drugs Black gave us hit him harder. I took a few shots with the girls so I was a little tipsy, nothing major. We were teasing him all night and before I came inside of the bathroom, Shay was telling him to take off his clothes. I lifted my mini purse closer to my face to get a better look inside, for some reason I couldn't find my lip gloss.

"Ughhh."

Knock! KNOCK!

Two hard knocks at the door startled me, causing me to drop my bag onto the floor.

"Shit!" I said opening in the door.

"You taking too long and he is knocked out cold! Let's go!" Shay yelled.

"I'm coming, I'm coming," I told her. Bending down, I grabbed all my items that were scattered on the floor that I could.

"Hurry!" Shay yelled.

Christina had Randy's wallet on her lap with all his cards on the table. Shay passed her the machine that Black gave to us. All she had to do was swipe the card and all the money from his cards would be gone and transferred into a secret account. "Come in the room with me so we can see what we can find!" Shay said.

Walking passed Randy; he was out cold with his hands tied behind his back with his tie that Shay took off of him earlier. Inside of his bedroom Shay was rummaging through all the drawers and closets trying to find stuff. "Here put these on," she told me handling me a pair of gloves that matched hers and Christina's. Lifting up the bed, we couldn't find anything. Shay started knocking down the portraits inside the room to look for a safe. "Why are you just staring? Do something!" She yelled. Stepping inside a walk in closet, I saw his wife beautiful clothes. *What a dog*, I thought. Taking her clothes off the racks, I threw them onto the floor. She had pieces of jewelry in the closet that I stuffed into my pocket.

"Wow these shoes is so nice," I said to myself picking them to see if they were my size. They were a half size bigger but I wasn't letting these babies get away. Sitting on the floor, I took off my black pumps to try them on and they fit perfectly.

"Did you find anything in here, I found the safe but it's locked," Shay said walking into the closet. "Damn, this a fly bitch," Shay said examining all the different attire. Looking down at my feet, she noticed the new pair of heels I had on. "I would say something but I probably would've did the same thing too, come on!" She yelled as I followed her back into the bedroom. Beside the bed was a small safe.

"Don't put in too many codes before it locks," Shay told Christina.

"Well what other option do we have but to guess? I got enough money off the cards; we probably don't even need this shit!" She said aggressively. Over the top of the safe was a picture of him and his wife on their wedding day with a date next to it. It's worth a try, but I knew he couldn't have been that dumb.

"Move over," I told Christina. I put in the same numbers that was on the date of the wedding picture. The safe indicted that was the wrong code, *shit!*

"Hold on, let me try," Shay said. She put the date of the wedding in backwards and the safe clicked.

"Yess!" Christina yelled. Opening the safe, it was stacks of money inside.

"Damn what kind of business you said he owned?" Christina asked.

"It doesn't even matter! We hit a gold mine!" Shay said excitedly. Stuffing our bags with most of the money we left out the room. Walking to the table Shay grabbed the glasses and bottles because our fingerprints was on them. Exiting out the loft, we got inside the unmarked car. After driving for a while, we changed our clothes inside of the car and then trashed it after wiping it down.

"Black said for us to meet him at a club in queens. I didn't know the name of it but he said he's sending a car to come and get us, "Shay said.

"With all this stuff on us?" I asked.

"Yeah, the bouncer isn't going to check us. We have to give the card scanner to one of his people's so he can hook it up to his computer and we'll get the money. Usually it's a check," she explained.

"Okay."

A few minutes later, a black Yukon pulled up. After confirming that was our ride, we got inside and he pulled off. Inside the car we counted the money and split it four ways, of course with Black getting majority of it. I wasn't complaining because I still came up with a healthy piece. We finished the rest of the Jack Daniels before tossing it on the side of the road. About thirty minutes later, we pulled up to Angel's nightclub in Flushing. Calling Black, Shay told him to come out because we were here. Walking to the front of the club, the bouncer asked for our IDs. Digging inside my mini clutch, I couldn't find it.

"Damn, I know I left the house with it," I said to myself.

"Didn't you have your ID to get the room for the Motel?" Shay asked.

"Yeah, I must have left it there or something, I don't know," I said now getting upset.

"They with me," I heard Black tell the bouncer. Looking from me to Black the bouncer let us in.

"Next time, have your ID," the bouncer said.

Fuck, where is it? I thought to myself.

Sophia

Do I really look like a dyke? I questioned myself looking in the mirror, taking notice of every feature on my body. My brown freckles decorated my face, as the years went by, more just appeared, which I got from my father because freckles were all over him also. I didn't have many curves but I think I had a little something, standing up; I turned around in the mirror.

"I don't think it's that small," I said out loud referring to my back side.

Turning back around, I walked closer to the mirror running my fingers through my fresh blow out. It was a heat wave outside so sweats were out of the question for me. I grabbed a pair of my red dolphin shorts that I got from Forever 21. I liked them because they looked just like sweatpants, but of course were shorts. *I must be gaining a little weight because it's fitting tighter than usual,* I thought. Finishing my outfit off with a white tank top and my red and white Converse. The sun was finally setting so I was ready to go.

"Okay, I'm leaving," I told my mother walking to her bedroom door.

"Okay baby, be safe," She tiredly told me. I knew she was exhausted because she just did a double. She was a nurse at a local hospital. She overdid it on the workload to keep herself busy. She was still battling losing my father, a few years ago he passed away from Cancer. When my mom got his insurance money, it was enough for her to not work for a while, but I honestly think she never even touched it yet. That was a long five years ago. After locking up, I put my headphones in my ear and started my walk. Melody didn't live to far from me so it shouldn't take me too long to get there.

*****

When I reached Melody's house, almost everybody was outside on her stoop just chilling. After greeting everybody I went inside to go get a cold bottle of water. I was drained from that walk in this hot weather. I walked towards Melody's mother, Jane's room to say hello. Knocking on her bedroom door, I realized she wasn't there. Her mother worked at the same hospital as my mother, that's how me and Melody became best friends. Walking passed Black's room; I heard the loud music he was playing on the radio.

"Hey Black, I didn't know you were here," I said standing at the doorway of his room.

"*Hey black,*" he said mimicking me. "Ain't no hey black, where's my hat?" he asked.

"Oh shoot, I forgot it home."

"Nah it's cool, I'm just fucking with you. It's hot as hell out there right?" he asked reaching over his bed to open his door more. He had on lime green Adidas track pants with no shirt on, like always. He wasn't buff, but he wasn't a twig either. The top of his crown was decorated with curls everywhere. Looking passed him onto his bed, it was money scattered all over it. I heard rumors of how he got money but I didn't really know if it was true. But then again, I never saw him with an actual job.

"Yeah, that's why I came in the house to get some water," I told him.

"Why you in here stealing waters? You got your hair done and think you all cute now I see," he jokes.

"Stop playing," I laughed as my cheeks flushed.

"Melody told me about you going away to school, instead of staying here, that's dope. I'm proud of you. It's always good to get a new experience."

"Thanks ugly."

Getting off the bed, walking past me, he went inside the bathroom directly across the hall from his room, leaving the inviting scent of his cologne close behind him. Turning on the light, Black started to run his hands up and down the side of his face looking in the mirror, while licking his lips, "who ugly?" he asked, turning his attention back onto me with a hard stare. Looking him up and down, I immediately felt a weird sensation between my legs so I crossed them as I watched Black, watch himself in the mirror. Looking down, I noticed my nipples were hard also, which was weird because it was very hot. I only wore a sports bra under my shirt so it definitely wasn't hard to notice. Crossing my arms in embarrassment over my chest, hoping Black didn't see it. *Why is this happening?* Looking up, I didn't have to wait for long to see if he noticed because he was staring at them also. Noticing I was looking at him, he brought his attention back to my face.

"So yeah. I'm going back on the porch with Melody, see you later," I told him as I rushed out of the house and away from him.

Melody

"About Time," I told Sophia.

"Sorry, I was just talking to Black," she said sitting down on my stoop next to me.

"Oh okay. So yeah, guess what?" I asked Sophia changing the subject

Giving me the side eye, she answered, "what?"

"So while my mother and Rob go away for their honeymoon trip next week, I'm going to tell Drew to come over," I said happily.

"And your brother? Did you forget about him?" she asked.

"Oh, I'm well prepared for that. He doesn't even come in my room without knocking first and he's barely even here. It will be the weekend, so he'll probably be occupying his time with a hoe or two," I told her.

"So what are yall plans? What are yall going to be doing?" She asked.

"Ummmm fucking for one! Duh Sophia, get in tune, but I don't know, just relaxing, watching Netflix, I can cook him a little meal here and there, show off my *wifey* skills or whatever," I said flipping my long lemonade braids.

"So how does it feel?" She asked.

"How does what feel?" I questioned.

"You know…. Sex."

"Well it feels good to me, but shit I am still a beginner, I think the feeling sometimes has to do with the heat of the moment or how you feel about the person," I explained.

"Heat of the moment? You mean how you feel before it happens?" she asked.

"Yeah, something like that," I responded.

"How do you know when you are in *heat?* You get weird tingly feelings?" She asked.

"Hold up, hold up," I said waving my hand, "Somebody got you all hot and bothered?" I asked her.

"Nooo," she shyly answered.

"You're lying! Who? Tell me," I pressed.

"Nobody Mel. I think that I'm just ready," she explained.

"Like ready, ready? Why? " I asked.

"I don't know, like a part of me just wants to get it over with before I go away to school," she explained.

"So you meant to say your hot ass is ready now?" I asked jokingly.

"Something like that," she said.

"You have anybody in mind? You don't even talk to anyone," I reminded her.

"Yeah I know, for me to just get it out the way, I don't think it has to be somebody I think I'm in love with. It's like eating me alive in the inside," she explained.

"Sophia, there's no rush. Now if you ready to pop it for a real nigga, I'm all for it. But, if you know for sure you are not ready, you can wait girl. You can find one of those fine college men that be stepping and shit," I said as we both laughed.

"No. No if ands or buts, I'm ready."

"Okay, okay the weekend my mother goes away would be perfect. If you feel like it's not what you want to do, just call me and I'll have Drew drive so we can come and get you. So who's going to be the lucky contestant?"

"What about Jah? Me and him is cool so I know he wouldn't go run his mouth. It's like a friend helping out a friend," she said.

"Jah, Jah? Girl he doesn't even seem like the type. I don't believe you're going to go through with this but let's see. This is going to be so funny," I said laughing.

"Go through with what?"

Turning around, we saw Black standing in the doorway with his car keys in his hands.

"Nothing nosey," I said as me and Sophia both giggled together.

"Yeah aight, I'm about to be out of here, don't stay out here too late. Sophia if you need a ride home, tell Mels to call me," he said walking to his car.

"Okay, so let me tell you how to start it off and finish," I told Sophia as we went over every detail, well shit, as much as I could give her.

*****

One week later...

"Don't be having all your hoodlum friends inside of my house, unless you call me! Or I will make Black come over here and check on you," My mother said walking to the door.

"Ma, really? You know I only be with Sophia," I told her.

"Yeah, yeah. I'm going to call you before I get on the airplane okay. If you need extra money, just call your brother and behave yourself Melody!" she said unlocking the door.

"Yes, yes, I know mommy. Be safe and don't forget to send me pictures," I said waving my hand as her and Rob walked to the car.

"Love you," she said waving goodbye.

"Enjoy!" I screamed waving goodbye.

Go time!

Running to my room, I grabbed my phone and texted Drew to see what he was doing.

Sophia

Okay Sophia, you can do this, I said to myself. Today was the day, the day that I thought I was ready for. I was so tired of everybody saying I was a dyke and believing that I liked females and what not. Tonight, I was going to have the last laugh. Also, I was curious as to how it felt too. Melody told me everything that I needed to do to get him started and I remember step by step. That night after leaving her house, I hit Jah up and told him I was coming over next week. I know he didn't think anything of it so he was okay with it. Sometimes, me and Melody went over to his house on the weekends when he had little gatherings. I would've told him to just come over, but it's no telling when my mom would come home so I didn't want to take that risk.

MELZ: *Remember what I told you, if you change your mind me and Drew would come get you!*

ME: *Yes, I know, I'm coming over right after.*

My hair was still nice from my wash and set so I put it up in a high ponytail. Grabbing my fanny pack, I told myself that everything was going to be just fine as I walked out the door.

*****

"So what are your plans for tonight?" Jah asked me rolling his joint. Jah wasn't a bad looking guy, so this little exchange should be a breeze. His hair was in the style Omarion made trending. The fade on the sides, with the middle braided up into a little bun. His eyes were kind of chinky, but he was always high so I didn't know if that was because of the weed or if his eyes were just naturally like that. He was rather on the short side, me and him being the same height at five three...

"Nothing, just going to go over to Melody house after."

"Oh cool, cool. Why she didn't come over here with you?" he asked me.

"I think she is going to come over a little later," I lied. *Damn why is he asking so many questions?*

"Oh aight, you want to hit this?" he asked me after taking a few pulls from the blunt. I wanted to but I didn't want to be high and fuck everything up. Smoking weed wasn't really my cup of tea anyway.

"Nah, I'm straight," I told him.

"I got some hen dog left over from last night, you want some of that?" he offered.

"Yeah fuck it, why not."

Getting up, he left out of his room to go get the alcohol. Looking around, he had the typical teenage boy room. The walls were decorated with blue painting. Shoes and clothes were all over the room like he just threw them anywhere when he took them off. Trap music was playing from his Play station two, or maybe it was his Xbox, I wasn't really sure.

"We just got lucky, my brother going to cop another bottle," Jah said coming inside the room with a half empty bottle of Hennessy.

"Oh okay, good because that bottle is almost done."

Maybe a little alcohol will make me feel more comfortable.

Melody

"When are you going to give me a baby?" Drew asked me rubbing my belly

"Baby? Boy please!" I laughed.

Drew and I were lying down, catching up on Power. It just came out this year in June and was the shit! 50 cent hit a number with this! I knew this show was only going to get better. Drew was my boo bear. We been messing around for a while now. In school, he used to annoy me so much. I even had my brother come up to the school to scare his ass straight one time. He still didn't give up, that's when the thought came to my mind that he liked me. I don't usually do the chubby boy thing but I love my teddy bear. I finally gave him a chance and we have been inseparable ever since. Drew has wanted to tell Black about us, I don't know why I was so scared but I knew he was bound to find out soon. Quite frankly, I was tired of the sneaking around too. I was grown! I think I should have a say so on who I --

"Shit, who is that?" I whispered to Drew.

"Aww fuck," he said grabbing his forehead.

"Ayo Mels!" I heard Black scream.

"Damn! It's my brother! Get under the bed!" I told Drew.

"How?" he asked with his hands out pointing to his body. Shit, I forgot he was a little on the chubby side that quick. I was not expecting Black to be here on the weekend. He's never here on the weekends! My mother must've sent him to check up on me.

"Just lay down on the floor in the corner then!" I told Drew. The way my room was set up, it was space between the bed and the wall so Drew was just going to have to make it work! Running to my door, I went to go open it.

"Why you took so long to come out?" My brother asked me.

"I... I just got out of the shower," I lied.

"Oh okay. I'm surprised you not outside with Sophia doing some ratchet shit. Where she at? She in the room with you?" he asked trying to come inside my room.

"No she's out!" I yelled.

"Out?" he questioned.

"Yeah she's ummm busy," I told him.

"Busy? Busy doing what? Why you not out busy with her?" he questioned.

"Black why you asking so many questions?"

"Because I want too! I feel like you up to something, so now I'm going to sit here until I'm ready to leave," he said going towards the kitchen.

"Ughhh! Why do you have to be so annoying?" I whined.

"I just want to spend some time with my little sister. What's the problem?" he asked.

Ding!

I heard my phone go off. I forgot I left it on the kitchen counter when I made me and Drew some food. Before I could even go and pick the phone up, Black went ahead and grabbed it before me.

"Talking about Sophia, she just texted you. 'You said all I have to do is start rubbing on his thigh first right?' Why the hell she asking you this?" He asked me after reading her text message out loud.

"Uhh--- I don't know," *Shit! Sophia is going to kill me.*

"You don't know? Okay well I'll refresh your memory when I tell ma you out here coaching Sophia," he said.

"OMG! Black! Ugh you get on my nerves," I yelled throwing myself on the couch, dramatically.

"Who thigh she rubbing on?" he questioned.

"I don't know," I mumbled.

"Yes you do. Why you got to be so secretive?" he asked.

"Why do you care so much?" I asked.

"Because I feel like it! Now tell me before I tell Ma and Sophia's mother," he said.

"But why Black? Just whyyyy?" I was getting so irritated. I swear I was never speaking to him again. He started to walk to the back of the house and I didn't want him to even attempt to go inside my room.

"Okay, okay!" I yelled. I didn't know why out of all days he picked today to be annoying.

"I'm waiting," he said.

"Okay, its Jah," I said, apologizing to Sophia in my head.

"Jah who's that?" he asked.

"Jah. Eric little brother," I explained.

"Oh word? Aight bet," he said walking towards the front of the house.

Yes! I'm glad he left! Oh shit! I forgot about Drew.

"Baby you okay?" I asked him rushing back to my room. Running to the corner where he was at, he was just staring at the ceiling.

"I am not ever coming back over here again!" he said angrily.

"It was not my fault! He left, you can get up now," I told him.

"I can't, I'm stuck!" he yelled as we both busted out laughing.

Sophia

Why isn't she texting me back? I wondered.

    I texted Melody over fifteen minutes ago and she still didn't reply. I was feeling the effects of the liquor and was ready to just get this over with. I was just confused on how to make the first move. I don't remember if she said to rub on his thigh first, or his arm. Ugh! Looking from his arm to his leg, I just went for it. Scooting over to where Jah was sitting playing his game, I grabbed his arm and rubbed on it.

    "Oh shit you noticed too? Yeah man I been in the gym getting money!" he said as he started to flex his arms. *What a loser? He can't see I'm trying to come on to him? Yeah maybe she said to rub on the legs first. Here goes nothing.*

Moving my hand from his arm, I put it on his leg. Taking his attention away from his television screen he looked at me confused. "Yo Sophia what you doing?" he asked. Suddenly, we heard a lot of noise coming from the living room. "Yo *Black*", "Was sup Black", "Yo I didn't see your ass in the minute", "Yo get Black a cup!"

Black? What the hell was he doing here?

"Yo Sophia you good?" Jah asked pointing to my hand on his thigh.

"I. uhh..." I was so focused on what was going on outside of the door, I forgot that I was still touching Jah.

Knock! Knock!

Someone started to knock on Jah bedroom door. He got off the bed, shaking his head, still confused about what I just did and opened the door. "Yo Black was sup!" Jah said giving him a five. Coming further inside of the room, Black was giving me a weird look.

"Was sup Soph," he said. *Ugh kill me now!*

"Hey Black, bye Jah, I am going to text you," I said getting my things before I walked out of his room.

Grabbing my phone, I immediately texted Melody.

ME: *Girl, why the hell your brother just showed up to Jah's house? I'm so embarrassed!*

Walking out the door, I ran down the steps. *Wow, I'm just going to be a virgin forever. Maybe that was a sign.*

MELZ: *I told him you were there, but I didn't think he would pop up. I'm sorryyyy.*

ME: *What??!!*

MELZ: *He came over here while Drew was here asking about you. He saw the text you sent to my phone. Hold on, I'm about to call you.*

"Sophia!"

Turning around, I saw Black in his car at the light. I hope Jah didn't tell him I was trying to come on to him. I would be so embarrassed. "Oh, hey Black! Just walking home," I said still walking with my head down. Pulling over to the side walk, he leaned over in the car to open the passenger side door. "Get in," he said. Nervousness filled my body as I sat down on the comfortable leather seats.

"Was sup with you?" he said.

"Was sup with me? Nothing just hanging," I replied nervously. My phone started to ring loudly from Melody calling me. I definitely wasn't going to answer the phone now. She would just have to wait until I get home.

"What you were doing with that lil nigga?" he said.

"Nothing just chilling, I was actually waiting for Melody," I responded.

"Really? She told me she was staying in because you were busy."

Shit!

"That's why she was taking so long, she must've forgotten," I lied.

"Oh okay. I thought you were over there rubbing up on thighs and shit," he said sarcastically.

"Rubbing on thighs?" I asked confused. I was hoping that was not the messages Melody was referring to that Black saw.

"Yeah, trying make first moves and shit. I didn't know he was your type," Black said.

"My type? What are you referring to?" I asked.

"Nah you good shawty. I thought shit like that would matter to you, I guess I just got the wrong impression."

"Shit like what?" I asked rolling my eyes.

"Niggas you out here fucking," he responded.

"Who said I'm fucking?"

"If you aren't, you were about to, with a living room full of niggas. Then, in a lil nigga dirty ass room. I didn't take you for the type," he said.

"Since you want to be all in my business, I don't know why it even matters to you, but I just wanted to get it over with, okay!"

"Get it over with? You just going to give something so precious? This not even you. Why the rush? You suppose to let it be with a nigga that care about you or something," he said focusing his attention back to me at the light.

"Do you care about all your 'home girls'?" Don't be a hypocrite telling me what it is that I need to do. I'm just tired of people thinking I'm gay or a dyke and I'm NOT!"

"So you were just going to give it up because of what people think?" he laughed.

"What's funny? You know what, I don't even care anymore. Just stay out of my business!" I yelled.

"Don't anybody want to be in that shit. You better be glad I cared enough, you good ma," he said pulling up to the front of my house. I opened his car door making sure I slammed it. I think this was officially the worst night of my entire life. Black didn't even watch me go in the house like he usually do, he just sped away. I was just going to cry myself to sleep for the rest of the night, I think I officially hated my life.

Sophia

A few weeks later...

"Hurry so we can go get some food," I told Melody right after I clocked out. Every Summer we volunteered at Brooklyn Methodist Hospital, which was where our mothers worked at. This was my last weekend here before I went away to school, finally. This was not the summer I would imagine and I was ready to go. It was bittersweet because I was going to miss my mother and best friend, but I could come home during my breaks so everything should work out just fine. After Melody clocked out, we walked out of the hospital to go find something good to eat.

"Are you coming over later?" Melody asked putting on her big round shades, like the diva she was.

"Yeah, I should be," I lied. Ever since that situation happened with Black, I stopped coming over to avoid him at any cost. He really hurt my feelings that night and I just didn't want nor need his negative energy around me.

"You say this every weekend and never come. Ever since my brother popped up at Jah house, you been acting weird. What happened that night?" she asked.

"Nothing happened and I'm over that situation, I just been so busy," I lied.

"Bitch, busy doing what?" she asked.

"Getting ready for college and stuff," I told her, which was half true.

"Okay just please come tonight, It's something I need to show you and I rather not over facetime," she explained.

"Okay, I'm going to come."

"Good, I promise it's going to be worth it," she said.

"Yeah, yeah whatever," Melody said as we walked into the nearby food court.

A few hours later...

After I got off from work, I went home to take a nap for a few hours. The crazy summer temperature was wearing me out. My plans were to come out once the sun went down so it can be a little cooler. Making my way to the corner of Melody's block, I spotted Black car. *Ugh! Doesn't he have somewhere to be? Let's just hope he left his car and isn't here.*

ME: *Come open the door I'm outside.*

A few seconds later, I heard Melody footsteps getting closer to the front door. "Hey beautiful," Melody said opening the door.

"Yeah, yeah, what's this big thing you got to show me that was just too exclusive for facetime?" I asked cutting to the chase.

"Okay, relax sister girl. Come with me to the backyard, I have something on the grill," she told me.

"See this is why I love you," I laughed. One thing about Melody is that she was always cooking something up. Walking closer to the back of the house, I can hear music getting louder and louder.

"Open the back door for me, while I carry this out," Melody told me. Opening the back door, I was in total shock.

"CONGRATULATIONS!!!!"

"Awwwww Melz," I said hugging my best friend getting emotional. Walking down the stairs, I hugged everyone that was here, or at least tried to. If I was aware of my surprise party, I would've worn something better than this, but it's not called a surprise party for no reason. I couldn't believe I didn't know what she was up to. Everyone that we knew from school was here and some people from around the neighborhood. Even Jah was here, somebody that I was ducking for a while now also. I couldn't believe I was eager to lose my virginity that I was going to throw myself onto him. Black didn't know it but I secretly thanked him. I thanked him, but didn't forgive him for the way he spoke to me that night. I know he saw me as a little sister also, but in all reality, I wasn't his little sister and he needed a wakeup call. Speaking of the devil himself, Black walked out of the back door. Always the one in bright colors, he had on a soft baby blue collar shirt that was wrinkle free and a pair of ripped white denim jeans. In his right hand, was a little wrapped gift box and a bottle of Hennessy in his left hand. "*Was sup Black*", "*Yooo*", was all you could hear in the background. Like always he stole the spotlight and got the most recognition. Rolling my hooded light brown eyes, I turned my body paying attention to whatever Melody was yapping about.

"Time for some shots!" Melody screamed grabbing my face and pouring who knows what down my throat. *Ew is this vodka?* Swallowing the shot, I felt the alcohol go down with a burning sensation. *No, this is definitely tequila,* I thought wiping the specs of alcohol from the side of my lips.

"Umm can you warn me next time? Thanks," I told Melody, finally able to speak.

"Don't be such a wussy," she teased.

"Why you been ignoring my text?" Jah asked me walking up to me.

Here we go, I thought. "I wasn't ignoring you, my phone is off," I lied. I felt bad for giving him mixed signals but nothing even happened, so I didn't understand why he was blowing me up, sending me weird text messages. If this what females went through with guys, just imagine how guys act after sex. Jah was giving me creep vibes.

"We still didn't talk about what happened that night, I'm trying to see where your mind at," he told me grabbing my hand, softly massaging it.

"I... uhhh... Look--" before I could come up with some kind of lie, my hand was snatched from Jah's grip.

"Lemme holla at you for a minute," Black said grilling Jah. Jah got the message and walked away.

"I just want to apologize if I made you feel anyway that night. I just see a lot of potential in you, so I basically spoke without thinking. What you do isn't any of my business. You just have been around for a little minute so I fuck with you," Black explained.

"It's cool, we good," I told him trying to dismiss the conversation. I just wanted to enjoy my party and not deal with these weird ass men.

"Don't be like that. Look I got you something," Black said pulling me in for a hug.

"Well now that I'm getting gifts and what not, apology accepted," I laughed taking the little box from him. Tearing the wrapper, I opened the box was surprised to see it was a diamond chain in the shape of a heart. Black asked if I wanted him to place it on my neck, and I told him yes.

"Do you like it?" he asked me.

"Yes, I really do. It's beautiful," I smiled.

"Yeah, now you can go back and talk to your little boyfriend," Black laughed walking away.

"He's not my…" I started to yell out, but stopped myself. I didn't have to explain myself to him.

A few hours later...

"When Black leave, I'm thinking…. Drew should come over again right?" Melody asked.

"Girl, did you not learn from the last time?" I asked.

"Yes, I learned to be more careful. You got to live your life with no regrets girl!" Melody yelled.

"Do you know what time your mother gets off of work?" I asked her.

"She's doing a double, how did you think I pulled this off?" She asked referring to the party.

"Ya know... I didn't even think about that," I told her sipping the rum punch Melody made.

"I'm going to miss you girl," Melody sadly said, putting her arm around my shoulders.

"Don't make me sad," I told her.

"I'm going to straighten up the backyard and take a shower. Can you go see if Black is getting ready to leave? He's overstaying his welcome," she joked walking away. The party ended some time ago and Melody and I was sitting in the living room just chatting and sipping. I was so thankful to have a caring friend like her. Walking down the hall, I stumbled into the wall. Laughing at myself, I knocked on Black door before walking in.

"I just came to thank you for the gift," I told him sitting down next to him on the bed. "Wow I never actually been here before, your bed is actually more comfortable than Melody's. I should sleep in here when I spend the night when you're not here. Actually it's bigger too."

"Well you are rather chatty, no more drinking for you," he laughed taking the red cup from me and putting it on the dresser next to the side of the bed he was lying on.

"Come on! It's almost done! Give me back my cup." Leaning over him, I reached for my cup that was beside him. Sitting back onto his headboard I took my drink to the head. "See all done," I told him putting the cup down next to me on the floor.

"I hope you know I'm not driving you home," Black said.

"Good, because I'm not going home."

"And where are you going?" He asked looking down at the watch on his wrist to check the time.

"To Jah house," I teased. Of course, I wasn't really going there but for some reason, the situation with Jah seemed to get Black a little upset.

"Oh aight," He said getting up. Pulling him back down onto the bed, I told him that I was just joking but by now, his whole aura changed.

"I was just playing Black; you know I'm going home. Can you drive me… please?" I begged him walking to the side of his bed he was sitting down at.

"Let me think about it," he said with an attitude.

"Come on, I'm tired," I whined trying to pull him up using more strength. Somehow I ended up falling on top of him on the bed. *Maybe I did have too much to drink,* I thought. "Oops, sorry," I laughed now face to face with Black. Trying to get up, he pulled me back down closer to him. "Stop playing," I laughed.

"Tell me you going to that little nigga house again, I dare you," he said.

"I told you I'm going home."

"You going to stop playing with me," he said, catching me off guard.

"Playing? What you mean by--" before I could finish talking, Black lips covered mines.

"Wait," I pulled back.

"Sssh, don't talk," he said grabbing my head bringing it back closer to his, kissing me again. I never kissed a guy before so I didn't even know where to start. *Fuck, I should've ask Melody about how to kiss!*

"What happened, you don't like it?" He asked me. *I didn't know what the hell was going on but I knew one thing for sure, Black was fine as hell and hell yeah I liked it!*

"I don't know how to kiss," I embarrassingly admitted.

"Just follow me."

This time around, I went in for the kiss. Pecking up my lips, I placed them onto his soft lips. I felt his hair from his mustache press against my face. With his lips, he sucked onto my bottom lip opening up my mouth a little more. I started to feel that tingly feeling I felt before. The feeling was becoming overbearing so I tried to stop him from kissing me, but that made him go harder. Black tongue slowly made its way inside of my mouth. I never knew kissing could ever feel this good. Moving his tongue around between the middle of my lips, I followed what he was doing.

"Damn girl," I heard him say very low.

Moving me from on top of him, he stood up. I saw a hard lump in between the middle of his legs. I didn't know rather to get up, or stay sitting on the bed. If this was the moment, I was going to make sure it went right. *The arm or the thigh? The arm or the thigh*? I couldn't remember which Melody said to do to make the first move. When I touched Jah's arm he didn't catch the hint so that leads me to think the thigh is right. Reaching out, I went and touched Black thigh, looking up at him. Grabbing my hand, he smirked and placed my hand to the middle.

"Why is it so hard?" I asked. Blacked laughed getting on top of me. He kissed my lips again and then went to my neck.

"You know I like when you wear your hair like this?" He asked me. I just had my usual style with my hair down from my wash-n-set I got again yesterday. Lifting up my shirt he massaged my breast before he went and sucked on them. The feeling was unexplainable. I squirmed under him to get him to stop.

"You want me to stop?" He asked.

"Yes please, it feels too good," I begged.

"I didn't even get started yet." He laughed getting on his knees. He slowly opened my legs wider. Grabbing the strings on my Dolphin shorts, he untied them.

"Wait," I told him.

"What I told you about all that talking?"

He pulled both my shorts and my panties down together. Taking each leg out, he grabbed onto them and placed them on top of his shoulders. Signaling me to be quiet he placed his pointer finger on his lips. Licking his lips, he went head first between my legs. Covering my mouth, I held it tight to muffle my moans. Looking up at me, Black was licking my clit with the tip of his tongue. Grabbing my legs tighter he kissed on it like he was doing my lips on my face a few minutes ago. Just from the lust in his eyes, I could feel the passion. The room was so quiet, you could hear the mess he was creating down below. Stretching his arms, he grabbed onto my breast and played with my nipples. I couldn't hold my moans in any longer. I didn't know what he was doing to me but it felt so damn good. I started to grind onto his face making sure to moan lightly. The hairs on his face was wet from me, or him, who knows. I grabbed the top of his head to try and move him, but he grabbed onto my legs tighter.

"Sophia!!" Melody screamed.

"Oh my god, Black please wait," I begged.

"Let it out, show me that I'm making you feel good," he said with a mouthful of my pussy. I didn't know what he wanted me to let out, but if it was this pressure I felt building up, I had to release it before Melody came looking for me. Grabbing his head, I pulled him closer as my legs started to shake. An unusual feeling took over my body, it felt like my inner soul was escaping from deep within. Getting off of his knees, Black leaned over and kissed my lips as my chest weaved in and out. That sobered me up real fast, and I realized what had just happened. Sitting up, I grabbed my shorts and panties off the floor. With a now weak body, I tried my best to quickly put my things back on, with Black watching me like a hawk. Finally gaining some better balance, I got off of Black bed stumbling a little for him to pull me closer to him.

"You know you're going to be mine one day?" he whispered into my ear. Grabbing my face, he gave me a deep passionate kissing before grabbing my butt. I ran out of the room to see what it was Melody wanted and to take my ass home. *I'm definitely not coming here anymore. I'm glad I'm going away to school.*

Black

"You look like you got something heavy on your mind, was sup?" Nino asked.

He was right, It was something on my mind, I was just confused as of why. Nino was throwing a pool party and like always, our crew got the most attention. The females were flocking on to us, not wanting to miss their shot of going home with one of us tonight. Don't get me wrong, it was a few I saw that I would've made that decision, but I just couldn't with how I was feeling.

"I'm good," I lied.

"Nigga you sure? All this ass standing around and you just staring into space. Here take a drink or something, shit."

Grabbing the bottle of henny just to shut him up, I poured some into my cup, mixing it with cranberry juice.

"That's what I'm talking about," he jokes "Yo, this is Jana," Nino said introducing me to a female that was friends with the female he was with. Giving her a head nod, she got closer to me.

"Do you mind?" she asked referring to sitting on my lap. It was no more seats around and her homegirl was sitting on Nino's lap so I didn't want to be rude and tell her no embarrassing her in front of her friend. "I'm not too heavy am I?" Jana asked once she sat on my lap.

"Nah you good shawty," I responded. Jana was one of those females with an invisible waist and a fat ass. Her face was decent looking, so she could pass for the time being.

"Oh shit, look who just walked in!" Nino laughed. Looking towards the back door of the house, I saw nobody other than my grown ass little sister and Sophia. I tried to get Jana off of my lap, but it was too late, Sophia already saw us. I couldn't really read her face, but I knew she was confused on how she should feel seeing Jana on my lap, considering what happened between us a few days prior. I wanted to get up and say something to her, but I didn't know if I had the right too, or even if she would had wanted me too.

"Blackkkk!" I heard my sister Melody call out once she saw me. *Shit!* I tried to move Jana off of me, but she wasn't getting the hint, or she tried to act like she didn't. I bet just her getting a chance to sit on my lap had her feeling like she won a prize possession. Finally reaching us, Melody and Sophia stood side by side in front of us.

"Who is this?" Melody asked referring to Jana, always being the one speak whatever it was on her mind.

"None of your business, what are you doing here?" I asked her, but looking at Sophia trying to read whatever it was going through her mind.

"To get in the pool, duh."

"Was sup Sophia?" I couldn't help but to say something to her. I knew the way things were looking probably ruined my chances of ever having anything happened between us too.

"Hey," she responded as if she had to force herself to say something to me.

"Anyways, were going to have some fun, we will see you later," Melody said.

"Ummm I don't think I'm going to stay long, for some reason I'm not feeling well anymore," Sophia said. I knew with what she just saw, had something to do with that. I wasn't going to let her go home without talking to her first. At this point, I didn't give a fuck about who saw us. My gut just wouldn't let me. I grabbed Jana to move her off of me.

"Yo!" I called out to them. Before I could reach them, I felt somebody grab my arm from the back.

"Who is that bitch?" Karma asked referring to Jana.

"Karma what the fuck do you want?" I asked turning around. As annoyed that I wanted to be, I couldn't help but to get a good view of the thong white two piece she had on.

"I take it as somebody like what they see," she said smiling.

"Nah, it's nothing I never saw before," I said not wanting her to feel like she had one up on me.

"Who was that bitch sitting on your lap?" she asked again.

"How many times do I have to tell you, you're not my girl, yo!" I yelled focusing myself back on Sophia and Melody. By now, I couldn't see them so I made my way into the house with Karma on my heels. Reaching the front, Sophia was standing outside with Melody. Noticing me, Melody spoke up. "Black there you go. Are you busy? Sophia said she doesn't feel well and need a ride home."

"Nah, I'm not busy," I responded.

"Excuse me?" Karma asked rolling her neck.

"You look busy," Sophia replied looking Karma up and down. "I'm good, my uber around the corner," Sophia said with an attitude.

"See she doesn't need a ride," Karma said.

"Karma would you just shut the fuck up sometimes? Damn!"

"Soph-" I called out before she cut me off telling Melody goodnight.

"Yo I'm about to dip, Melody you not staying here let's go," I told her. Once I dropped Melody off, I was going straight to Sophia house. I couldn't fight the feeling anymore.

"Can you take me home too?" Karma asked.

"Did I drive you here? No," I told her walking to my car.

"Ugh Black. Why do I have to leave too?" Melody whined.

"Your ass should've never been here in the first place!" I yelled.

Getting in the car, Melody slammed my door with an attitude. "It was a mistake," she said before I could even say anything. I knew it wasn't but I was going to let her rock for the time being. After finally dropping Melody off, I got back in the car and made my way to Sophia house. I had her number, so I was just going to tell her to come downstairs. Turning the corner, I noticed the police behind me, blinking their lights for me to pull over. *Shit, I must have been speeding,* I thought. Little did I know, they had me right where they wanted me.

Melody

Four years later...

"I cannot wait until you get back. My life is so boring!" I complained into the phone to my best friend, Sophia. Her original plan wasn't to come back home, but she changed her mind. I was so proud of her for getting her degree like I knew she would.

"What happened to the boutique you was supposed to get started?" she asked.

"Ugh, I changed my mind. It's not what I want to do anymore," I told her. It honestly wasn't. Every time I get different ideas in my head, it would be a good start, but then go downhill.

I didn't do four years of college like Sophia, but I did do two and got my associates for Business Administration. I just got tired of doing the same ole thing and needed something new and exciting after a while. Just like my damn love life.... Once the cat was out the bag about me and Drew dating, it got boring. No more fun sneaking around, just the same thing year after year. He was my first real thing so I never got a chance to experience anything else. I always wondered what if's.... But that was just thoughts in my head because I never stepped out on him physically, only mentally. The summer when Sophia went away to school was when everybody found out about us. My mother caught Drew in the house the night of that pool party. Before Black could even confront Drew in person, like I knew he would, he got locked up. Even though he got on my last nerves at times, he was still my best friend and that crushed my heart not being able to see my brother every day. I heard about the things he did in the streets, but he never did any of those things around me, so who knows, it could've all just been rumors.

"Hey baby," Drew said walking into the house.

"Hey," I dryly said, sipping some wine from the glass.

"What's wrong with you?" he asked picking up the wine bottle shaking his head.

"Did I say anything was wrong?" I asked snatching my bottle away from him. He always complained that I drank too much. It's only wine, he's acting like I'm sitting here taking shots of vodka or something. Matter of fact, he complained about every damn thing I did and I was getting tired of it. Going in the kitchen, he pressed the start button on the microwave without looking into it. I was heavy on cooking so he knew he would have a meal every night when he came home.

After the food was hot enough, he took the plate out and went to sit on the couch to eat his food. He held the food closely to his face while scooping some up with a spoon every few seconds. This was the same ole bullshit that I was tired of. He would come home, eat, and then take his ass to sleep. I never got any of his time or energy. It was boring and most importantly draining. *Ugh, I need another bottle*, I thought getting up and dragging my feet towards the bar. I needed to rack up on some more bottles because my stash was getting smaller. Grabbing the bottle of Pinot Grigio, I walked my ass up the stairs clenching my wine opener in my left hand. I needed something on the strong side to get me where I needed to be. Drew was going to fall asleep right on the couch like he did every night.

Sophia

I lied and told Melody I was coming home next week but I was already at the airport ready to get on my flight last time we spoke. I went over to my mother's house and surprised her also. It felt so good to be home and knowing I'm not within a time frame. Don't get me wrong, college was an experience I would never take for granted. If I could, I would do the whole thing over, especially with my best friend right by my side, but she had other plans. Which I'm so unsure of now. During the four years I was gone, Melody was all over the place. Everything takes time so she would find herself soon enough.

Knocking on Melody's house door, I covered the peephole. I knew she would be home because she didn't work.

"Who is it?" she yelled from before the door. I didn't answer but just continued to knock. Getting upset, Melody swung the door open with an evil grill decorating her face. Realizing it was me, that grill was now a sad grin. Her emotions showed all over her face. We embraced into a hug with both of our eyes filled with tears.

"Look at youuuuu Nurse Mitchell," Melody said looking me over. "I thought you were just hitting good angles on Instagram but yes my best friend got booty now," she continued turning me around while I blushed.

"Alright, alright that's enough," I told her walking into her home, now feeling myself. I haven't been back home to New York in four years. On my breaks, I could've come home but I decided not to because that's how people got distracted and I wanted to finish college with the same energy I had when I first started. I saw how depressing my roommate would be when she came back home after seeing her family and I didn't ever want to go through that. I was now a registered Nurse and that was the number one goal.

"That's what good dick would do to ya," she said slapping my butt. *Only if she knew*, I thought. I felt bad for lying to my best friend about my sex life but hey, at this point, I was embarrassed. I was literally a twenty-three year old virgin, twenty-three! It wasn't meant for me to have sex so I gave up trying. I had a few in counters here and there while away at school, but each time something drastic would happen, so I said fuck it overall. Men were a distraction anyway, so I really didn't care to be in a relationship. My main focus was just getting my degree. Now oral sex, I wasn't a virgin in that department. Ever since Black did what he did to me years ago, I yearned for that feeling again. Silly me, I thought another man could get me to that point, but I was fooled. It wasn't anything compared to how Black made me feel that night, but it was good enough to make me have an orgasm so I was cool with that.

"I have so many things planned for us to do before you start working, you staying here right?" she asked me.

"I don't want to get in the way, I'll probably stay with mom until I find me an apartment," I told her.

"Girl, Drew is barely here and I just am so lonely, pleaseeee," she begged.

"Okay, okay, just until I get on my feet," I told her.

"Let me go get us some wine, so we can play catch up," she happily said walking off.

*****

Two bottles of wine later, Melody came up with an idea to go to a nearby lounge she went to a lot. So here we were at the bar talking up a storm. Well that was until a brown skinned guy came up to Melody to buy her a drink, offering me one also. He definitely was not hard on the eyes and caught both of our attentions. He had a dangerous appeal to him, but once he smiled while talking, it magically disappeared. One drink turned into more drinks and at the point we were living our best life.

"Don you are so funny," Melody laughed rubbing his arm. *I didn't think he was that funny, but whatever.* Don excused himself and walked away to answer his phone.

"I haven't been this happy and so long. My best friend is back home, my brother will soon be home--"

"Soon? How soon?" I cut her off, I didn't know Black was coming home soon.

"I didn't tell you? He's coming home next week! We are having a welcome home party for him! You came back home just in time."

I never told Melody what happened between Black and I. It didn't go too far and I didn't know if he would want me to, so I kept it to myself. Soon after, he got locked up so I left it as a distant memory. I didn't know where to go from there and we never talked again after that. That night left me confused. Anyways, that was years ago so I knew I didn't have anything to worry about now....

"Yo, I got something to handle, I'm about to shoot out of here. Maybe we can meet up and chill again?" Melody's new friend, Don asked her after walking back to where we were.

"Yeah, that would be cool," Melody suggested.

"Bet. Here put your number in my phone and I'm going to hit you." Passing Melody his phone, she stored her number in. Giving me and Melody a hug, Don was on his way.

"You think it was a good idea to give him your number?" I asked her.

"Yeah, it's nothing wrong with having a male friend. I'll probably won't even meet up with him anyway."

"Yeah, that's true," I agreed with Melody.

"He was fine though!" She yelled out while we both laughed. I couldn't deny that. He was the best eye candy that we had all night.

One week later...

Tonight was the night of Black welcome home party at a club named Blackout. I decided on wearing some jeans and a nice blouse. On my feet was my favorite pair of loafers. Over the years, I was far from the twig I once was. Puberty hit me ten times late but it was fine. Besides working, I was consistent with working out to get the body I wanted so that was a plus for me. My long brown hair was also gone. I now had a short red pixie cut that complimented me well.

"Okay I'm ready to--" Melody said walking into the room.

"What?" I asked her confused.

"Girl… what the hell do you got on? You look like a damn grandma. I said we were going to a club, not to church," she said.

"You are dragging it, I always go clubbing like this," I told her confused turning around looking back in the mirror.

"Well not with me! Oh lord," she dramatically said holding her head.

"Well what am I going to do now? It's too late to try and find something Downtown."

"Hold on, hold on, let me think," she said walking into her closet. "I got a few outfits that are too small for me, but I still kept it because god willing I might lose some weight," she said. A few minutes later she came out with what looked like pieces shoe strings sewed together.

"I'm not wearing that," I told her.

"Once it's on you, it looks better, I promise you," she said.

"Melody but whyyy, please find something else."

Going back into the closet, she came out with something that was worse than the first outfit! The dress was see-through everywhere. *What the hell kind of clothes did she have?*

"Just pass me the stringy thing!" I yelled getting upset, taking off my clothes.

It was a hassle to get the dress on, but once I did, I wish I never put it on. Looking from the mirror to the see-through dress on the bed. It looked like this was my only option. The black dress I had on covered the front and my backside, but the sides were out connected by a string. The style reminded me of shoelaces on sneakers.

"Wow look at you! They going to want to fight you tonight," Melody jokes.

"And I got the perfect shoes," she said passing me a pair of shoes with the slimmest heel I ever saw in my life. "What you thought you were wearing those ugly shoes of yours with this dress? Got to be kidding me," she said, shaking her head.

"I cannot walk in heels Melody," I told her.

"Well you better learn tonight because we are leaving in ten minutes," she said grabbing her bag.

Black

    Damn it felt good to be a free man. Jail wasn't for me and I damn sure wasn't going back there. But, with all the shit I was doing in the streets, I rather had got caught up for this little charge than anything else. I look at it like a blessing in disguise. My man Nino came to get me once they released a real nigga. The first place I stopped at was my mom's crib. That was my number one lady, and I'm glad to still have her in my life breathing and healthy. Now the second stop, was to get me some damn pussy. Four fucking years using my hands, I didn't even want to see those shits anymore. Karma was on a nigga for four damn years, so that's where I went. When I first got to her crib, she wanted to sit down and talk but I didn't have time for any of that. She called me all the time when I was locked up, we talked enough over the years. After giving her all the rounds I had in me, I lay down in the bed trying to relax but I realized that was only wishful thinking. Karma started to guard me with one question after another. It was my first day home; I didn't have time to deal with her so I was making this visit short. I had shit to do today anyway.

"So what does this mean?" she asked.

"Come again?" I asked her confused putting on my shit.

"You fresh out and you here with me, so what are we official or something now?" she asked.

"Didn't you say you got some pussy for me when I come home? Fuck you talking bout Kama?"

"Yeah... but I thought."

"You thought what?"

"Four years I gave you. I thought when you came home, we can start working on us."

"For one, I never asked you for shit. Second, I don't know where you come from with that stupid ass idea because I damn sure never gave you those type of vibes. Third, I'm out because you on some dumb shit," I told her grabbing my car keys.

"Black, wait, I'm sorry," she cried.

"Imma holla at you later," I told her walking out the door. *These bitches be bugging out.*

****

"Yo Black was sup," a guy came up to me giving me a pound. He looked familiar, but at this point, I didn't know who he was.

I was getting mad love in the club. This shit was on point too. *I should get into the club business*, I thought. The niggas was showing love, the bitches, even the club owner Nas. I was loving all this shit, I'm finally a free man, damn I was thankful. I was a Black nigga but I always stayed in some fly shit. It was the middle of spring and with New York's weather that meant it might still feel like winter and shit. I had on a pair of Butta's fresh out the box. I didn't know what niggas was out here wearing lately but I had a few people do some shopping and shit for me before I came home to keep me up to date. On my body was a pair of black Amiri jeans and a white collar Gucci shirt with the snake design on the collar. Being locked up without shit to do most of the time, I took that opportunity to work out. I was never a frail nigga but I was definitely far from that now. My goal wasn't to look like those big diesel ass niggas but I damn sure did look good.

"Blackkkk," I heard somebody scream. Turning around, I saw it was my baby sister Melody. A nigga was hyped up to see her yo! Back in the day, she gave my ass a headache but love is love. My lil sis was a grown ass woman now! She ran up to me and hugged me. I felt nothing but love from her energy. I couldn't control the smile that was plastered on my face. As I'm hugging my sister, I saw the girl she was with struggling to walk with some heels on, up the stairs to enter the section.

"Melody that's it! I'm never wearing these damn heels again!" I heard a familiar voice say.

"Yo who you got with you? Go help her ass before she fall," I laughed.

"Boy, that's Sophia ass," Melody laughed.

Sophia?

Sophia

Why the hell did we have to walk up some stairs? I thought to myself as I struggled with each step. Melody just threw me to the wolves after she ran off. She helped me the whole way over here, but now I was on my own. I was already on one nervous as hell to see Black. I don't even know why I was nervous in the first place to begin with. That was four years ago for crying out loud. That man probably wasn't even thinking about my ass. Finally reaching the top section, a guy walked up to me.

"Damn who you here with ma?" he asked me looking me up and down making me feel uncomfortable. *I knew I should've never worn this,* I thought to myself wrapping my arms around my body. Before I could speak, I felt a pair of eyes on me.

Looking up I finally saw who they belonged to. As Melody ran her mouth to him, his attention was focused just on me. A feeling I haven't felt since I was a teenager suddenly came back to me. I know they say the milk does a body good, but damn I think jail does a body even better! Fuck the dress Melody had me wearing, I felt completely naked now with the way Black was staring at me. I ran my fingers through the top of my head fixing my pixie curls that I felt was out of place. The guy in front of me was talking but I couldn't hear anything he was saying. Noticing Black wasn't paying her any attention, Melody turned around to see where his attention was focused on.

"Sophia, hurry up and come say hi to Black!" she yelled.

On top of not being able to walk in these damn shoes, and feeling like the shy teenager I once was, I proceeded to make my way towards them.

"Damn, you just going to walk away from me?" the guy asked pulling my hand.

"Hold on, I'll be right back," I told him.

Finally in front of them I let out a fresh breath of relief. *Get it together girl.* Black extended his arms out to give me a hug. Coming in for the hug, "hi Black," I shyly said. He wrapped his arms around my waist, as I relaxed my head on his chest. It felt so good to be in his arms, the feeling was unexplainable.

"I like your haircut," he whispered in my ear and I swear my knees got weak. I know he just gave me a compliment on my hair but damn if it didn't feel like the best thing ever spoken. Before I could thank him, I heard somebody clearing their throat.

"Ahem, excuse me."

Looking up, it was a face I would never forget his *homegirl*, Karma. Ruining our embrace, I unwrapped my arms from around him and gave us enough space. Looking me up and down, I knew she was trying to remember where she knew me from.

"Come on Sophia lets go get some shots to take with Black," Melody said grabbing my hand. Karma looked from me and Melody, finally recognizing me, she started to laugh.

"Nooo," she dramatically said. "I know this isn't your little sister's friend, the little dyke," she laughed. Melody looked her up and down and before she could respond like I knew she would I grabbed her hand. "Let's go," I told her walking away. Of course luck wasn't on my side, because I damn near broke my ankle. Karma was laughing like it was the funniest thing in the world.

Black

    With Karma parading around like she was my woman, and Sophia over here looking good as shit, I couldn't focus for the life of me. I wanted to curse Karma ass out but I was trying to enjoy my night without the drama. Sophia ass had me adjusting my dick every few seconds. I don't know if it was because I just got out of jail, or what, but I wanted to snatch her little ass up. The only thing was I didn't know where shawty mind was at, so I had to play my position. Some nigga that was in my section, that I didn't know was breathing down her neck. I was going to kick him out, but I didn't want to make it hot. Shit, that probably was her man or something. I'll let him have his time with her because the shit was definitely borrowed time now. Right on que, Sophia got up most likely to go to the bathroom because everything you needed was inside the section. I knew it would take her a while to get there with them damn shoes, so I was going to sit for about four minutes before I went to go find her. After taking another shot with Melody crazy ass. I made my way to the nearest women's bathroom.

"Where are you going?" Karma asked me.

"To go speak to somebody I know," I told her walking away hoping she didn't follow me.

Waiting outside the bathroom for five minutes, I was losing patience about to just go ahead and knock on it. Finally walking out of the bathroom, looking like the most beautiful girl in the world. From what I could remember, Sophia wouldn't dare wear what she had on, but I guess over the years things change. Females was outside of the bathroom so instead of waiting in front of the bathroom for her, I was at the end of the hall watching her. She didn't even notice me, as she walked past me singing the song that was playing in the club.

"Beautiful can I talk to you for a minute?" I joked walking up behind her.

Turning around, the frown on her face immediately turned into a smile. "Why you play so much?" She asked stopping, showing off her beautiful smile. "And why you sitting here by the bathroom by yourself? Oh you were waiting for *your home girl*?" She asked emphasizing on homegirl.

"Nah I was waiting on you," I replied honestly.

"Yeah okay," she said, obviously taking me as a joke.

"Nah I'm for real," I told her grabbing her hand pulling her closer to me.

"Why you waiting on me?"

"With homeboy up there not giving you a chance to breathe, I knew this would be my only chance to get you alone. So, how have you been?" I asked her.

"Pretty much fine, I just got back from school," she replied leaning onto the wall.

"Oh congratulations, that's was sup. I got to get you something."

"No it's okay, you did enough," she laughed waving her hand.

"Enough? What you mean by that?"

"You know what I'm talking about, matter fact, don't mind me, I'm talking too much." Before she could move from her spot on the wall, I got in front of her and leaned onto her chest.

"I didn't do enough yet," I whispered in her ear. Turning her head to face me, I went ahead and kissed on her pink soft lips that I wanted to all night. I can tell she was shocked from my reaction but she didn't stop me either. "I'm going to catch up with you later," I told her walking away, I'll give her some time to get her mind right before I stake my claim.

Melody

"Are you sure about this?" Sophia asked me.

"Yes, I am *sure* about this, what's the worst that could happen?"

Me and Don were going to hang out today, that's what I called it, but Sophia swore it was a date. I made sure to let him know that I didn't want to go anywhere local, of course for obvious reasons. Me and Drew was having problems at home, but I wouldn't blatantly disrespect him. I was bored and needed some male attention, Drew should've been doing his job. Sophia car just arrived from getting shipped to New York, so I had her drive me to meet him. I couldn't be that messy and have him meet me at my home that I shared with Drew, whenever he was there. She drove me to a close by park and we went from there. Don got out his Silver Audi, looking finer than the first time we met. Me and Don was only physically around each other one time, but when he started begging and pleading to spend actual time with me, I finally gave up. A man hasn't cared enough to try to make me feel special in a long time. Everything was on point with him, down to his Balenciaga shoes. I didn't really like those sneakers, but he made them look good. Being a gentleman, he walked over to Sophia car, opening the passenger door for me, and taking my hand. *Wow I don't remember the last time a guy opened the door for me.* Cheesing like no tomorrow, Sophia just was grilling away. *She'll be aight.*

****

Sitting down at the Chart House in New Jersey, I had a wine glass in my hand as usual. Me and Don sat patiently having small talk before our meal arrived. The questions he was asking me, I was rarely asked. He asked about my goals in life, my favorite color, even my favorite kind of music. Men these days didn't give a shit about that. Don was trying to get deep in tune with my spirit and figure me out. In my heart I knew this wasn't right, but at the moment it felt so good for someone to have an interest in me. As I took sips of my wine, Don grabbed my hand from across the table and caressed it, telling me to never doubt myself with anything in life. Every morning he would send me a motivational text that had me looking at the world different. Now I felt like I had a purpose in life. Starring me in my eyes, Don golden eyes stared deeply into my soul. I wonder if he knew I felt broken inside. What was the reason he came into my life, especially at this time? As if he could read my mind, he asked me, "Do you think everyone who comes into your life is for a reason?"

Sitting my glass down, I thought before I spoke, something I haven't done in a while, "why do you ask?"

"I don't know, I feel like you need me, like I need you. I know your situation and I'm not trying to get into that, but I'm saying just for comfort. I want to be your sanctuary if you let me." Catching my confused reaction, "I'm just saying, as a friend, whatever happens in the future, we cannot control," he clarified.

"Boy you crazy," I laughed nervously downing my wine. Saved by the bell, or should I say food, I was thankful it arrived because this conversation was getting very deep.

After dinner, Don dropped me off close to home, while I took a cab the rest of the way. Of course, he rather drop me off in front of my home to make sure I got there safe, but after a quick debate, he finally settled and told me to call him as soon as I stepped foot in the house. Putting my key into the door, I walked into my home with the biggest smile on my face that I haven't had in a long time. I just felt so high off of life. Taking out my phone, I quickly informed Don I made it inside safely.

Don: *Didn't I tell you to call me?*

Sighing, I took out my phone to call him. "Hellooo," I sang into the phone.

"I can't make sure you good?" He asked.

"What's the difference between a text and phone call?" I asked him unhooking my heels one by one with the phone to my ear, multitasking.

"It's a lot, once your man knows you good ma, and then that's when he's good."

"Man?" I questioned.

"You know what I mean Melody, you were my company for the night, so I got to make sure you as good as when I left you," he said.

"I understand, I understand," I agreed just to shut him up.

"Did you enjoy your night?"

"Actually I did, I haven't went out to have dinner in a long time." I admitted.

"That's no good ma, never settle, that's time you can't get back, remember that."

Looking at the kitchen, Don words spoke to me, I ended dinner early with Don, just to have dinner ready for whenever Drew get home. *Fuck that*. Turning away from the kitchen, I continued my conversation with Don walking up the stairs to the bedroom.

Sophia

Walking to my car out the hospital, I felt good about my interview, I knew I was going to get a job as a Maternity Nurse. That was my dream, but now I was making it into reality. During the four years I was gone, a lot has changed in New York, physically wise. Mentally, I know the people was still crazy. Starting my car, City Girls was blasting through the speakers playing on the radio. They were all the way ratchet, but the people loved them, I lowkey did too. A weird number has been calling me for a few days now, I ignored it hoping it wasn't one of the lames that I left up at college. My phone kept ringing interrupting the music that was playing from the radio annoying me. Pulling over, I took my phone out of my bag to block the number. *I should've been did this.* Somehow, I mistakenly answered the unfamiliar number.

"Damn girl about time, I thought I was going to have to come to Melody house and kidnap your ass," A man's voice boomed through the car speakers.

"Excuse me?"

"How was the interview?" the caller asked. Finally recognizing the voice I laughed to myself.

"Black how did you get my number?" I asked.

"From my big mouth ass sister, how else?" he responded.

"Figures, well thanks for asking, the interview went well. I'm feeling excited about it," I told him.

"That's was sup. I'm glad to see you chasing your dreams. So what you are about to do?"

"Nothing, go over to Melody house and relax," I told him.

"Hurd, I'll be over there later to see you."

"To see me, for what?" I nervously asked.

"A nigga trying to spend some time with you, what you mean? You been ducking me since the night of the party. Don't think I haven't noticed whenever I come through, you be missing in action. You ass can't be that tired every time I come by." *Hell yeah I get into hiding when he comes over to Melody house, his energy that be passing over to me is too much.*

"Yes I am a little tired as we speak," I lied.

"So come take a nap over here."

"But--"

"Girl just bring your ass, nobody trying to bite you, scary," he laughed.

"Ain't nobody scared," I spoke up.

"So prove it," he said hanging up. A few seconds later I received a text with an address attached to it. Spending a little time with Black won't hurt.

*****

Releasing a breath of relief, I got out of my car and walked to the front of the beautiful building, I'm guessing is where Black lives. Last time I checked, he had an apartment in the hood. Before I could even take my phone out to tell him I was outside, the door on the first floor opened. Black stood in the doorway, with a white T-shirt and a pair of white basketball shorts on, looking like a tall glass of milk. "Was sup shorty?" He greeted me pulling me in for a hug. *God, why does he smell so gooddd?*

"So this is my little spot, make yourself comfortable," He said closing the door. *Little? This apartment was kind of huge.* Going into the kitchen area, Black came back with two bottles of water in his hand. Walking towards the couch, I sat on it waiting for him to sit next to me. Once he sat on the couch, Black reclined the chair back and wrapped his arms around me.

"Was sup Soph? Why you been ducking me?" he asked cutting right to the chase, not being the kind of man to beat around the bush.

"No, I haven't" I lied.

"You sure about that?"

"I have just been a little tried you know," I lied again.

"Aight, imma let you have that. Where my kiss at?" he asked.

"Kiss?" I asked.

"Yeah, I didn't see you since the party and my lips are in need of some attention," he said smirking.

Grabbing his face, I puckered up my lips planting them on his cheek "Muah! Happy now?" I asked laughing.

"I'll settle for that," he responded grabbing the remote. "You still watch those romantic lame ass movies?" He asked surfing through the channels.

"Aw you remember, yes I do," I laughed.

"I remember everything about you pretty, and with you and Melody trying to make me watch them shits all the time, how could I forget?"

"True, true," I laughed.

"You seeing somebody?" he asked me.

"No."

"Okay good, I don't need anybody getting in my way."

"In your way of what?" I questioned.

"Us, I told you, you were going to be mine one day. Time took us away from each other for a while, but everything happens for a reason. I'm not trying be all up on your toes, I'm giving you, your time. I know you changed these past years, as well as me, so I'm definitely not trying to pressure you. I wanted you before and I want you now, so I'm going to leave it up to you."

"Why me?" I asked him.

"What you mean why me? Why not you? You smart, you funny, and you beautiful as hell. No lie, I wasn't aware of how I felt about you, until I almost had to grab your ass out that little nigga room. Yeah I didn't forget about that. After that night, I couldn't get you off my mind and no shorty ever made me pissed like that, for real. So, I started telling myself it's because *'I care for you like a little sis.'* But nahhhh, the night of your little surprise party, was when I became fully aware of how I felt. I couldn't believe your little ass had me on you like that, shit scared the hell out of me, word."

"Four years went by, you never reached out to me when you were locked up," I reminded him.

"Ma, when I come to you, I got to come to you with my shit well together. Not half way, because I don't expect the lady I'm dealing with to be halfway with me. You know what you deserve, and it definitely wasn't no nigga locked up." he admitted.

"I respect it, now that you say it that way," I told him.

"So what we going to do is, get to know each other, you know, date and shit, we can send each other little cute text messages. I'll tell you good morning and goodnight, you know that cute little shit you females like. You with it?"

"Welllll, you aren't that hard on the eyes, so maybe," I joked.

"So can I get my kiss on my lips now? Or I'm going to have to wait?" he asked. Finally giving in, I responded with a kiss to his lips.

and I knew he was getting fed up. It's been going on two months now and we still haven't had sex. *Maybe I should just tell him?* No one knew about me and him, well no one that I knew of. Yes, I really do like him, but I just feel like I don't fit within his caliber. I barely knew how to dress at times and I'm still a damn virgin. Who wants a virgin, seriously? Maybe it was an insecurity thing, but I just wasn't ready to go out in the public with this. My mind was racing a mile a minute and Black sexual glances weren't making it any better. *Ugh I need a drink!* Getting up, I walked inside Melody house praying Black didn't follow me. He respects my wishes with playing it safe, so hopefully he did tonight.

"Beautiful can I get some of your time real quick?" A guy approaching me asked following me inside the house. He wasn't a bad looking guy, If I wasn't seeing Black, I would have given him some of my time just for the fun of it. "I know you don't know me, but I heard it's your birthday, so I just wanted to tell you happy birthday face to face," he continued.

"Thank you," I quickly responded.

"You're Melody's friend right?" He asked as I nodded my head yes. I didn't want to be rude but he was definitely barking up the wrong tree. "So any other plans you got for the weekend? If you don't have any, I would like to at least take you out. My name is Qua, and yours is Sophia right?" he asked.

"She ain't interested."

Oh boy. Black came inside the house staring me down.

"How you know that Black?" Qua asked taking a sip of his Heineken. I didn't feel any tension coming from either of them, so they must have been cordial, which was a good sign.

"You know what, you're right. Well are you interested Sophia?" Black asked me smirking.

"Sorry Qua, I'm not interested," I responded politely.

"Man, I ain't ever see you go hard for your sister like that, cock blocker," Qua jokes walking back towards the backyard door.

"See what I mean? If these niggas out here knew you was mines, what just happened wouldn't ever be a thought. Why we sneaking around like little kids and shit. What is it? What you embarrassed for people to know you mines or something?" Black asked cornering me up by the counters.

"No baby, I just need time."

"Time for what? What you scared of? You think I'm going to hurt you or something? You should know by now the feelings I have for you ain't no fake shit." Lifting me up, he rested me on the counter top. "What is it? I'm not cute enough to be your boo?" He laughed nuzzling my neck.

"Baby you know you sexy," I flirted massaging his arms.

"So when you going to stop playing and stop hiding me like I'm some whack nigga?" Black asked now replacing his nose with his lips. "You don't know how bad I want you, I don't think I can wait any longer, ma. I need to be inside you." *Oh trust me I know,* I thought.

"I want you too." I wasn't lying, I really did think I was ready for the next step but I just didn't know how to come out and tell him. "Wait... Black... what are you doing?" I whispered as I felt Black tugging at my panties under my skirt.

"Didn't you just say you wanted me to? Lift up, before I rip them off."

"Wait... what if Melody come and see us?"

"Don, why would you think—"Melody said to Don before looking at me and Black realizing she might be caught. "Oh, there she is, hey Sophia, your cousin Don was looking for you," Melody nervously lied. She was so caught up in her own mess, she didn't even realize me and Black was alone in her kitchen with his pants unbuttoned, and my flushed cheeks. Helping me off the counter, Black went about his business while I went to get my "cousin".

Melody

Your call has been forwarded to....

"Well then fuck you too!" I screamed after ending the call. This nigga has the fucking nerve! He's been ignoring my calls for one whole week after the barbeque fiasco. Don is upset because I told him what he did was wrong. Because it was! He only confirmed he was coming over to drop Sophia's gift off and to see me for a little while, not stay basically the whole night playing cards with Drew. I may have lied to Sophia, well not lie exactly, just deny the truth about Don liking me. The more I denied it and friend zoned him, I felt he would finally get the picture. I was texting him that whole night telling him it was time for him to go, before he finally said his goodbyes. I lied to Drew and told him I was walking Don to the door but I really wanted to speak my mind about the situation. That was until, I was almost caught by Sophia and my brother Black. I never got a chance to tell Don how I felt because he blocked me right after that.

"I'm coming, I'm coming!" I yelled walking down the stairs to whoever was behind my house door ringing the bell like a maniac. Looking through the peephole, I saw it was Sophia behind the door in her pink scrubs doing the pee-pee dance. I should've let her suffer more for the way she just up and disappeared most of the time, but I have to realize we are not teenagers anymore and we both have lives to live. Well her, my life was basically consumed up in this house alone.

"Oh, look what the wind done blew in," I said as she zoomed past me to the bathroom ignoring my pettiness.

Sitting on the couch, I grabbed my phone to entertain myself until Sophia was done in the bathroom. A bright idea popped up in my head, I searched Don's instagram to see what he's been up to this week, but I couldn't find it. *I know he didn't stoop that low and block me on instagram too!* Rolling my eyes, I forcefully threw my phone onto the table. With Sophia gone I really didn't have anybody to talk to and Don was kind of my go to person. Now I see, the feelings definitely weren't mutual.

"Look what I got us," Sophia said walking out of the bathroom with a bottle of wine. Of course, my favorite. I knew she was trying to butter me up, I sure wasn't complaining.

"Oh how nice." Grabbing the bottle from her, I went into the kitchen to get the wine opener. "So when are you going to tell me about the guy you're dating?" I yelled from the kitchen. Of course Sophia ignored me. I grabbed us two wine glasses and proceeded back to the living room area. "You didn't hear me?" I asked pouring us both some wine.

"No sorry I was reading something, what did you say?"

"The guy your dating? Who is he?" I asked her getting straight to the point.

"His name is Jimmie; I promise you'll meet him soon. Me and him are taking it kind of slow, I don't want to let it out in the open and it's a complete bust."

"Hmph. Well okay I guess." I felt away she was keeping secrets from me, but I guess I understood her reasoning. "Let's just say, if you had a friend and they randomly cut you off, after speaking to each other every day, would you feel away?" I asked her.

"Yes I would, but it all depends on the situation at hand," Sophia said looking at me suspiciously. I didn't share with her that Don blocked me because I didn't want to hear her feedback, which would be the truth that I just didn't want to face.

"Can I see your phone real quick? My service has been acting up," I lied. Going into her purse, she handled me over the phone. Going straight to instagram, I searched Don's instagram and clicked on his page. Low and behold, I was definitely blocked. Going to his story, he posted a female hand under his, and he was bold enough to put the location. Now, I can give a rats ass about who he spending his time with but he owes me an explanation.

"We should go grab something to eat," I told Sophia. Yeah I was going to go and grab something to eat alright. The nerve of this dude!

"Do you see what I got on?" she asked referring to her scrubs.

"You act like you don't have clothes here, hurry up I'm hungry!" I lied.

I was already dressed so I didn't have much to do but wait on Sophia.

"Wait. I'm just confused. What don't I get? Why do you feel as if we shouldn't be friends anymore? I miss you, I miss our conversations, I'm lonely," I sadly admitted.

"Mann," he annoyedly said massaging his temples. "Conversations huh? Aight I'll give you that. Anything else?"

"A hug?" I sorrowfully asked with my arms out. Coming closer to me, Don pulled me in for a hug. I haven't received a male's physical attention in so long; I felt my knees getting weak. His cologne that invaded my nostrils made my mouth water. "Ima hit you later aight," he told me kissing my left cheek. I felt it was a little too close to my lips, but maybe I was bugging. I was just overwhelmed with excitement to get my friend back.

Black

Today I decided to do a good deed and take Shay crazy ass to look at new homes. Since being gone for four years, Shay wasn't the tough fuck love kind of chick anymore. Her ass done settled down and was working on baby number two and wanted to look for bigger homes. While I was away, she put me on game how she found a nice guy and the whole nine yards. What she forgot to mention was that the nigga she found was white. Ain't nothing wrong with biracial dating, but Shay? Nahhhhh, I would've never seen it coming. Looking at her rub her protruding belly just reminded me of how my ass isn't getting any. I know all about that awaiting trial period women be trying to force men to do. I figured that's what Sophia was trying to do. I'm not trying fuck up what me and her got going on so that leads me abiding by her rules and shit the best way I could. I ain't fuck nothing else since Karma, and that was when I first came home. I've been gone for four damn years; Sophia could've at least given me one night! First it's her period that seem to be going on for longer than usual, she blamed it on her birth control, which she have no control over how it affects her body so that's fine. When she complained about not shaving? I realized see she's playing fucking games with me.

"Ayo, when you first got with your man, you made him wait a few months for y'all to fuck?" I asked Shay turning the radio down.

"No, actually it happened pretty fast. And, we did not *fuck*, we made passionate love, thank you," she replied flipping her hair.

"Aight bet, good looking." I responded turning up the music just for Shay to turn it back up.

"Why? Who got you on probation?" Shay jokes, trying to pry in my business like always.

"Don't nobody got me on no damn probation," I lied.

"Sounds like it to me, let me find out you lost your spark by being locked up. You better hit Karma ass up for a quick fix," she laughed.

"You got jokes right? Now I should make you walk your big ass the rest of the way home."

"See why you got to push it so far? At least I'm getting some, can't say the rest for everybody else," she mumbled going into her phone as I stopped the car because of her slick ass mouth. "Ugh Black, I'm just playing! You really must be backed up! Whoever she is that is making you wait most likely just wants to take it slow with you, or honestly she's fucking somebody else," Shay honestly told me. Sophia don't give me any vibes that she's fucking anybody else, she knew better, or so I thought.

*****

My sister was cooking dinner tonight, so we were all cooped up in her crib waiting for the food to be done. Sophia didn't know I was coming, so she was surprised to see me when she arrived in her scrubs looking sexy as hell. Melody was in a good mood today and I wondered why. Coming from upstairs, Sophia was now changed into some tight ass leggings and a tank top. Walking towards me, she sat down onto the sofa next to me and kissed me.

"You missed daddy huh?" I asked her lifting her and placing her right onto my lap.

"Yes, I missed you," she whispered into my ear.

"Sophia did you--" Melody come from inside the kitchen, catching Sophia off guard with her little scary ass, she jumped off my lap and fell onto the floor.

"Sophia what's wrong with you?" Melody asked looking at her with confusion.

"Oh nothing, I'm just looking for my earring, it slipped out of my hand," Sophia lied.

"Oh okay. Well, I wanted to know if you wanted me to make you a to go plate for your boo that you be with every other night?"

"Uhh yeah, thanks girl," Sophia responded waving her off.

"I'm right here," I said while Sophia gave me the death glare.

"Huh?" Melody asked confused.

"Nothing."

"Boy you crazy, Drew is almost here so don't worry. I wouldn't want you to get bored with just us here annoying you. Sophia can you come help me make the plates?" Melody asked returning back to the kitchen. Sophia got off of the floor and made her way to the kitchen with Melody. Well, not before I gave her ass a slap. I was tired of playing these games with her, real talk.

Melody

"A toast to wealth, happiness, and success," I said raising my glass in the air.

"A toast?" Sophia asked confused.

"Yes, that's what they do in the movies," I laughed.

We were in my backyard chilling after having dinner, of course sipping some wine as usual. Well Sophia and I, Drew and Black were on the other side talking about whatever guys talked about. I loved my home and my life, it just felt like something was missing. More like excitement was missing. Glancing at Sophia, she was texting away on her phone just blushing. I miss the days Drew use to make me blush like that. *Sigh*.

"So this guy Jimmie must be a keeper right?" I asked Sophia sparking conversation.

"Jimmie?" She asked confused. "Oh, oh, Jimmie, yeah girl I told you that's bae," she responded.

"Can I see a picture of him?" I asked.

"Uhh... he's not into social media like that."

"Well tell him to send a selfie! Let me see how my brother in law looks."

"Okay, I'm going to tell him to send it now," she replied.

Buzz!

Grabbing my phone off the table, I read the text message that just came through.

DON: *Come to my house.*

ME: *Your house?*

DON: *Yeah, didn't you say you miss a nigga?*

ME: *Yeah I miss you but… how am I just going to leave my home this late alone? Drew is here.*

DON: *You on lockdown or something? You can't get up out the crib to come see a friend? I thought you were tired of being cooped up in the house not doing shit.*

ME: *I am.*

DON: *Hurd. Make it your business to get over here.*

I was so engaged with the back and forth texting between me Don, I didn't even see Black and Drew standing over us. Locking my phone, I tried to act as normal as possible even through on the inside I was squirming.

"I'm about to get up out of here, Sophia you still need a ride?" My brother Black asked her.

"Awww this is just like the old days when you use to drive her home from mommy house," I laughed. "What's wrong with your car?" I asked her.

"It's been acting up a little for some reason. Hold on Black, let me go and get my things," Sophia said.

"Wait don't forget your plate of food for *Jimmieee* and you still didn't show me a picture of him!" I screamed out.

"Jimmie? Who the fuck is Jimmie?" Black asked.

"Sophia boo! Mind your business," I laughed hitting him on the shoulder.

"Boo?" Black asked a grill. Pulling out his phone his sent a fast text before walking towards the backyard door. "Yo Melody I'm out," he said disappearing into the house with Drew behind him.

"Wasn't you leaving with him?" I asked confused. Sophia looked at me confused also looking into her phone.

"Maybe he's in a rush to go somewhere," she said shrugging her shoulders to sit back down.

"Well good, because I can just leave with you," I responded getting up.

"To go where?" she asked.

"Just to hang with Don for a quick second, we need to have a talk to get all this shit straightened out," I tried to convince her.

"Why can't you just take your car or even a lyft?" she asked with an attitude fast texting on her phone, not even looking up at me.

"Well damn, alright I'll just do that," I told her rolling her eyes.

"My bad, something just came up, come on let's go and just know, whatever it is that you plan to be doing tonight or whenever, I have nothing to do with this shit," she said getting up.

What was up with everybody tonight?

*****

I told Drew I was going with Sophia over to her mother's house for a quick second. He didn't think nothing of it so everything went as planned. Sophia dropped me off at Don's house and drove away with an attitude. I don't know if it was because of where I was going or what, but If it was, she didn't have to put so much damn thought into it! And for the record I was grown so this shouldn't be any of her concern, she act like I was fucking Don or something. My relationship honestly didn't have anything to do with her, nor did this have anything to do with my relationship. I just liked Don's company. Why did she make it seem like it was such a bad thing?

Walking to his door, I rang the bell. I have never been inside his home, so this was going to be my first time. A few seconds later, he came to the door shirtless, with a pair of black denim jeans that hung below his butt and a pair of black Gucci slides with a blunt hanging from between his lips. His mahogany frame towered over me. Looking me up and down, he licked his lips before pulling me in for a hug, inhaling my neck. "Was sup ma?" He greeted me after embracing me.

"Hey friend," I smiled walking into his home. It was more like a bachelor pad with not one ounce of a woman's touch. He was watching a basketball game with the huge flat screen television on mute with music blasting in the background. I sat on the brown leather recliner chair, while he sat on the loveseat.

"Why the hell you sit your ass all the way over there?" He asked me.

"I don't know, this chair looked comfortable so that's why I decided on this one. What? You want me to sit over there with you?" I teased.

"Bring your sexy ass over here and stop playing with me," he smiled showing off the bottom grills in his mouth looking so thuggish. Getting off the couch, I glided over to him.

"So that girl you were with, that's your girlfriend?" I asked.

"Nah just a female friend I decided to occupy my time with," he responded sparking his blunt.

"Oh okay, she's aight," I told him.

"Nah shawty bad," he laughed.

"Maybe to you."

"Why are you hating?" He questioned.

"Me hating? I just want what's best for my friend and I personally feel like you can do better."

"Do better with who? Somebody like you?" He questioned.

"That's not where I was going with this conversation. But if you must know, yup," I laughed.

"Why can't it just be with you then?" He asked me.

"Here you go," I laughed.

"So then don't question me if you not ready for any of the shit I got to say."

"Yeah okay, you got anything in here to drink?" I asked him.

"Yeah go make yourself comfortable in the kitchen," he responded sitting back with his legs cocked wide open. Getting up, I went to the kitchen to see what he had in the fridge. Of course being the kind of guy he was, I saw tons of beers and a few bottles of water. I decided on a beer for now.

"I'm not staying long, all I came over here was to tell you, your little girlfriend was ugly to your face," I laughed. Pulling me down over him, he kissed me on my lips and then bit my bottom one taking me by surprise.

"Don... wait why did you kiss me?" I asked pinching the sides of my lips.

"They were looking juicy so I wanted to know how they felt," he responded nonchalantly.

"Well you cannot do that because I have a man and you know what."

"So then you why you came over? Tell me was sup. Let me know what's on your mind."

"I just came over here because... I don't know because you told me," I responded. "Actually I don't know why I'm here; I'm not supposed to be here." I said out loud but rather to myself, getting up I walked towards the door.

"So you're just going to leave? Before you go sit down real quick and let me talk to you," Don said. Sitting next to him, I took a sip of my beer waiting to hear exactly what he had to say. "I'm going to give you some time to get your thoughts together but I'm not going to wait too long. You knew what the fuck you was doing and I don't understand why you running from it. When we are together it doesn't feel good? It doesn't feel right? I let you go and do you a favor and blocked your number and you came running back. Why did you? Just cause we're friends? You don't feel anything more, tell me you don't and I'll let you go right now," he said rubbing my inner thigh. His hands were moving higher up my thighs.

"I'm waiting Melody, tell me I'm not what you want," at this point his hands found its way inside of my panties and his mouth found the side of my neck. I wanted to tell him to stop, I wanted to get up and leave like I intended to. Instead, I stayed on the couch and let Don have his way with me.

Sophia

ME: *Baby it's not what you think…. it's nobody else but you, I just made up a name to Melody because she noticed I haven't been around a lot. Can you text me back please?*

Read @ 10:05PM

Black was officially tired of my games and I don't blame him. I should've been honest with him about everything. At this point, I don't even know why I was still trying to hide our relationship from the world. It was obvious that he wanted me, I don't know what I was so scared of…. At this point, I knew I needed to get my shit together before he really be done with me. Last week, we were at his place and his phone was ringing while he was in the shower. Now, I never go through his phone because Black never made me feel insecure. Curiosity did get the best of me that morning and I happen to cross upon his messages. It was different female's names all up and down his messages begging for some of his attention, only one name stood out to me, *Karma*. Things like this made me just second guess myself in his life, not in an insecure way though, if he had all this pussy just one phone call away, why is he sitting here hand and feet waiting on me? And, why was this bitch still contacting him? We never brought her up, but she's been lingering in the background for a few years now. This weekend was going to be the weekend it finally went down. I got waxed down there and brought some lingerie. I was going to give Black my virginity. *Was I ready? I think I was ready...*

Here goes nothing.

I sat inside my car, debating if I should go and knock on his door or not. I was scared of what I may see on the other side of the door, but then again, I felt I had no reason to be. I knew he was upset with me, but I was hoping he didn't switch up that fast. Getting out of my car, nervousness took over my body with each step I took. Reaching the front of Black's door, I rang the bell. A few seconds later, he opened the door with a phone to his ear with a mean grill plastered on his face. Like always, he was shirtless with looking fine as wine. It was impossible he always looked so sexy. I couldn't let this thing go.

"I thought by me ignoring you, you would get the message. What you doing here?"

"Can I come in?" I asked sadly.

"For what?"

"So I can explain what happened."

"Explain what? How you want to play these little girl games? Or how you got caught up tonight? Which one exactly?"

"First of all, nobody got caught up tonight. If you had just let me explain, instead of up and leaving, you would have known there is no Jimmie! Granted, I know I've been playing games with you but I'm ready now." Black looked me up and down laughing as if I just told the funniest joke in the world. Pushing pass him, I walked into his place examining it to make sure nothing or someone was lingering around.

"Yo, Ima call you back," Black said into his phone.

"Who is that?" I asked referring to who he was speaking to on the phone.

"It's Jimmie," He responded sarcastically.

"Quintel, please." I responded calling him by his real name.

"Now I'm Quintel?" he smirked shaking his head. "So what is it that you want?" he asked walking up to me. His tall frame towered over me. His cologne filled up my nostrils with each step he took closer to me. "Tell me what you want," he demanded. I didn't feel myself backing up with each step he took closer to me until I felt the cold wall on my back. He grabbed my chin and forced me to look into his eyes. The look in his eyes were foreign to me, I couldn't exactly read them. Leaning down, he kissed me with his full irresistible lips opening up my mouth while his tongue got in between my lips. My heart started to speed up along with my breathing.

"I... I want you," I finally got out.

"In which way? Why I got to do all this to prove myself to you? What you scared of? What is it that I'm not doing right? Tell me so I can fix it. Do I scare you?" He asked interlocking his fingers with mines. His stare was strong and intimidating.

"No baby, I just..."

"You just what?" he asked kissing me again.

Taking his hand, I guided him to his bedroom. Slightly pushing him down onto his king size bed, I got on top of him. Palming his head with my freshly done French manicure hands, I kissed him with all the passion I had built up in me. Black hands slowly made it to the bottom of my ass, massaging it. I felt him harden under me while I continued to make love to his lips with mines. After I was done, my lips made its way to his neck. I spelled his name out with my tongue adding a little bite and suck here and there. Leaving little pecks on chest, I got closer and closer to what I was craving for. "Tell me how you want it," I told him grabbing his dick getting on my knees. I wasn't surprised by the look of shock that appeared on his face because I never done this before. Grabbing the waist of his sweatpants, I pulled them down. I grabbed onto his dick and stroked it. Moving closer, I opened my mouth and put the head inside of it, moving my head up and down slowly. This was all new to me so I didn't know if I was doing it right, looking up, Black was looking down at me biting his bottom lip as I forced more of him into my mouth. Making him feel good, was turning me on so much, I didn't even know this was possible.

    Wetting up his dick with my saliva more was making it easier to please him. Black grabbed the back of my head and fucked my mouth. Not in an aggressive way, but in a way that had me yearning for him to do the same exact strokes inside of me. Relaxing my jaws, I took more of him into my mouth, now he officially was touching the back of my throat. Working my mouth while Black guided me I grabbed onto his member while sucking harder. The moans that was escaping his mouth almost made me feel like I was about to explode instead of him. Suddenly, he sat up and removed himself from inside of my mouth. Grabbing me off the floor, he threw me onto the bed. His eyes were filled with so much lust and desire, desire to have me. Sliding off my leggings he went head first between my legs. His chocolate arms were wrapped around my golden legs. Fuck taking it slow, Black was demolishing me like I was the sweetest taste in the world. The feeling was so intense, I couldn't take it. I told him to slow down, but my begging fell upon deaf ears because he didn't pay my pleading any mind. The way he was pleasing me was so pleasurable I felt my eyes watering. Before I knew it, I finally let go and let out what I was holding in. Screaming out in pleasure, I released onto his face. I felt my essence escape out of me and make a pathway onto the bed. Trying to regain my composure and catch my breath, Black helped me out of the rest of my clothing. Getting on top of me, bare naked, skin to skin. I felt Black trying to position himself inside of me.

"Wait," I yelled out catching him off guard. Giving me his attention he looked up confused. "I don't know how to tell you this, but..... I'm a virgin," I finally let out. Black tried to get from on top of me, but I pulled him back down before he can say anything. "No, don't stop, continue…. I want you, I want this, and I want it all."

"You sure?" he asked. I could tell he was a little thrown off by my little secret I decided to share. I nodded my head, giving him the okay to continue. "Okay. If you want me to stop, just tell me. This is all about you right now," he said kissing me on my forehead. It was kind of cute and romantic that he cared so much, but I was backed the fuck up and was ready for it! He rubbed himself up and down the split of my opening to coat his dick with the remaining wetness I had still oozing out of me. Spreading my legs more, Black took it as que to try and fit inside of me. Holding my breath, I felt him breaking into me. Finding its way to embrace the inside of my walls. "Do you want me to stop?" he asked. Once again I shook my head no, giving him the okay to keep on going. Our eyes was lost within one another, our bodies was sweating with anticipation to have each other, minus the pain I was going through at the moment, I was almost positive pleasure would soon come after. Wincing in pain, I felt him getting deeper and deeper until he was fully in.

"Damn girl, you know this pussy is mines right? I just marked my territory," Black moaned into my ear while he stroked slowly. The pain no longer felt the same as it did before, but I still felt quite a discomfort, but the sudden pleasure was now filing in that void. Grabbing my breast he gave each of them a kiss before giving his undivided attention to my left one. Licking around my nipple, he then latched onto it while still stroking back and forth inside of me. I moaned into his ear as my body went through different motions trying to keep up with unfamiliar feelings that were taking over me. "You like that? Show me how much you like it baby," Black seductively told me in my ear. His movements increased faster as my moans grew louder. Grabbing onto his back, my nails dug into his skin.

Leaving evidence of what was taking place. Black was doing everything and more tonight, leaving me with no regrets.

Karma

    I put so much into this plan, for it to blow up in my face. Everything that I thought would happen when Black finally come home, went completely left. His first day home? He came to see me and fucked me like me missed me! Then just dip because he thinks I'm wilding. I'm wilding?? Me?! I held him down for four years while he was locked up and this is the thanks that I get? Play with mother fucking karma and your ass will damn sure get burned! I knew I should've told those cops more information on his conniving ass! Yeah, I told! So what! I damn sure wasn't getting arrested behind that mess. I tried to blame it all on Shay, but they knew she couldn't be the mastermind behind it. That was the first and last time I ever did anything like that, I'm not complaining though because the money was good, real gooddd. The cops found my ID that I magically lost that night and came questioning me with one question after another. Don't get me wrong, Black got some good D, but not good enough for me to take that bid for him so,

I sung like a bird. Once he got locked up, I felt good. I didn't have to chase his ass around; I knew where he would be all damn day and night! Technically, I did him a favor, he needed to sit his ass down before something worse was to happen to him.

    I was currently sitting inside my car, waiting for the clear to knock on his door. He actually never told me about his place, I just did a little investigation, or stalking, but whatever, at least I knew where he laid his head. The first day I came, I saw a girl coming out of his place, I couldn't really get a good eye, but I saw him kissed her goodbye. As long as I knew Black, he never ever kissed me. Maybe one day on a drunk night years ago but never sober. I felt away and tried to get a good look at the female, but she had on shades and scrubs. Probably was a fake ass nurse because I knew he couldn't be messing with an actual nurse. She had the same car as before, that was currently parked in the front so I knew it was her here again. It's cool because just like clockwork she was leaving approximately at ten in the morning like she always does, and now it was my time with Mr. Black himself. Still wearing shades, she entered her vehicle. She must be ugly because it wasn't even that sunny. Power walking to the front door, I rang the bell waiting for him to answer. I heard his footsteps moving quickly from outside the door.

    "You must have wanted some more dick before you--" Black started to say but stopped once he noticed it was me. "What the fuck are you doing here?" he asked. The smile that was first plastered on his face was now an evil grill, smile or not, he still looked sexy as ever. His white briefs fitted his body so sexy, but his big print was even more sexy. Catching a good view, I starred just one second longer, before my eyes got to his waist, taking a picture inside of my head of his V-line. Getting higher and higher, his sculpted body had my mouth watering with anticipation.

    "I came over to see what was the reason why you weren't answering my phone calls and now I got my answer." I said now staring back into his eyes.

"Okay, so why are you still standing here?" he rudely asked.

"Can we talk?"

"Talk about what?"

"So this is how you niggas do now, huh? Just use females while locked up for all they got?" I asked trying to make him feel bad.

"Bitc-- Karma, I ain't ever ask you ass for shit!"

"And you damn sure didn't stop me either! I thought me doing all of that proved to you that I can be the woman you need. I showed you that I can hold you down, no matter what!" I yelled. He started laughing like what I was saying was a joke.

"What the fuck is so funny?"

"So you don't think I know about the people you had relations with while I was away? The niggas you were fucking? What about the nigga's that you fucking now?'

'I... but..."

"Exactly! Pop your ass back over here and watch the fuck I do! Don't forget that I know everything. I dare you to tell somebody where I live and I will kill your ass," he whispered into my ear. This was the closest we have been in months and I felt a shiver down my spine. Turning around, I walked towards my car after he closed the door into my face.

Wow, so he's worried about who I'm fucking? Ha! I knew he cared about me, I thought smiling on the way to my car.

Melody

Two weeks later...

DREW: *Where are you at?*

DREW: *When you get home we need to talk.*

ME: *Talk about what?*

DREW: *Melody, don't make come looking for your ass.*

    Staring in a daze into my phone, I wondered what Drew wanted to talk about. Did he know about me hanging with Don? It couldn't be any way possible. The way things were going with me and Drew, I knew this had to be him breaking up with me. Honestly, I wasn't even upset because quite frankly, I felt as if it was over too. Things just wasn't the same with me and him anymore and sometimes that just happens. People just grow out of one another. Me and Don was sitting on his couch watching a movie before I told him to get up. I've been here almost every night and I honestly don't even think Drew noticed that I was gone. He probably didn't bring his ass home either. Pulling me back down beside him, he gave me a questionable look.

"Where you going?" he asked.

"Home real quick," I responded.

"Home?" Don grabbed the nape of my neck, turning me to look at him.

"Yes! Home!" I yelled pulling away from him. Don nose flared up as soon as he heard my response. Grabbing my phone, he looked at the text messages between me and Drew in pure disgust. Pushing me off of him, he made his way towards the door with his black basketball shorts sagging off his bottom.

"Since home is where you want to be, make sure to never bring your ass back here," he told me as I made my way outside the door. Before I could fully make my way out of his house, he slammed the door hitting me with it. If his ass was to just let me explain, he would know that I was going to cut it off with Drew officially. Oh well, I'll see his ass later. He's just in his feelings like always. Taking out my phone, I texted Drew and told him I was on my way.

*****

On my way home, I called Don over five times but yet again he had me blocked. Rolling my eyes, I drove into the driveway dreading this talk me and Drew was about to have. Apart of me didn't want to hear the exact words that it was "over", because really who does? I just wish we could've just let time go by and distanced ourselves from one another more.

Putting my key into the door, I walked inside. The sound of my heels clicked on the wooden tiles as I proceeded to follow the red roses that made a trail into the dining room. *Is this how people break up now?* Standing beside the table was Drew, in and all black button up shirt and pants. The diamond rope chain on his neck was glistening as if the light was shining on it. Now, I was really confused.

"What is all of this?" I asked. Without responding, Drew grabbed my hand gently and pulled me close to him. We haven't been this close to one another in so long, I forgot how good it felt. How good it felt to feel the warmth of his body on mines. Before I can begin to ask again, Drew placed his index finger onto my lips.

"It's my time to talk, come sit down."

Listening to his command, I sat down in one of the dining table chairs. Pulling a chair beside me, Drew took a seat also. Silent took over as I got prepared for what I thought I was ready for.

"I've been hearing you," he finally let out.

"Excuse me?" I asked confused.

"I've been hearing you," he responded.

"Been hearing me say what?" I asked.

"I have been hearing you complain, complain to me over and over about the same damn shit. I started to get immune to it, immune to hearing you complain but I wasn't listening. I wasn't listening to your needs as a woman. Your needs and your wants I was supposed to guarantee you. As your man, your provider, your everything. I've been slacking and I could admit that. I got used to this shit and I'm sure you did too. I let the shit I got going on in the streets get in between me and you. Baby, I'm sorry,"

Stunned, that was the only feeling I could describe right now. I thought I was walking into a breakup. "Wait, so you still want to be with me?" I asked confused.

"Baby I know we're not the same teenagers from years ago. I know I lost all that baby fat and shit, but I'm still your teddy bear," he told me leaning closer to kiss me on my cheek making me smirk. As we got older, he was not the chubby guy that I first laid eyes on.

"Drew, baby, but I --" cutting me off, he planted a kiss onto my lips.

"Baby you don't got to talk no more, you don't have to complain no more. I promise I'm going to get it right and if I don't you can leave me okay. I love you girl, whatever you want to tell me it's not worth it. All I need is a yes or no."

Seeing Drew get down on his knees was a scene I thought I would never ever see in life. All these years I gave him, everything I ever wanted was happening right in front of my eyes. Was this a dream? Maybe I should tell him now about Don and see if he still wanted me.

"Drew I have to--"

"Melody, it's either a yes or no," he repeated again.

The guilt was taking over me, I tried to tell him two times but he wouldn't let me get it out. Maybe I should just leave it in the past where it belongs. My heart was thumping; my nerves were bad, I was sweating even though we had central air in our home. Would I be wrong if I said yes knowing what I did behind his back? He said nothing matters and that's all that matters!

"Yes baby, I will marry you," I told him as he got off his knees and kissed me. Kissed my pain away, my mistakes, my deceit. All the guilt I felt went out the window was we made love on the dining room table.

The next evening

I woke up in such a high bliss. Looking down at the ring on my finger, all I could do was smile, smile because I for once in a long time, felt peace. When I accepted this ring, I let everything in the past go. My love for Drew never disappeared. I regret letting Don get all up into my head, I was better than that! I should've made it work with my man! Everything happens for a reason and my secret was going down with me into the grave. Getting out of the bed, I heard Drew talking to somebody, most likely on the phone because he always lets me know if we were having company over. Last night, Sophia swore up and down she had something to tell me so we were meeting up when she got off of work. Going into the bathroom connected into our master bedroom, I turned on the shower so I could get inside and hurry before she kills me.

Deciding on my knee high black suede boots and a brown knitted sweater, I was ready to go. I recently just got my long box braids done, so I just decided to put it in a bun which helped show off my gold hold earrings. Checking the time it was almost six and Sophia gets off at seven today. Grabbing my bag, I closed the door to the bedroom still hearing Drew big ass mouth talk on the phone. Grabbing the stair rail because I be damned if I fall in these heels, I made my way downstairs one by one.

"Baby I could hear your big mouth all the way upstairs," I yelled walking towards the living room where I also heard the television blasting.

"My bad baby, I was talking... Damn where you going looking like that?" he started to say before he realized all this sexiness that just appeared.

"To meet Sophia at her job. Now what were you saying?" I asked giving him as kiss.

"Oh, I said I was just talking to this nigga here, you remember Don right? Sophia cousin?" I swore my mind was playing tricks on me. Looking towards the bathroom where Drew was pointing, I saw Don come out of it wiping his hands with a paper towel.

"Oh shit, this your girl Melody right? Long time no see," Don said walking up to me and Drew. The air that I had in my lungs was escaping with each breath that I took. I couldn't believe what was happening right now, it felt like I was about to go into hibernation.

"Ummm hi," I responded nervously.

"Girl? Nah this my finance now! Mel come show him that fly ass rock I put on your finger last night," Drew gleamed.

"Fiancé? Last night?" Don asked. Drew may have thought that was excitement coming from Don, but I knew otherwise.

"Baby, I really got to go before Sophia kills me," I told him walking towards the door, not knowing what the hell I was going to do, or how the hell I was going to drive feeling like this.

"Yo let me go and get my other phone from out the car! I will be back!" Don said right when I got to the front door. I tried rushing out the door, but my palms were so sweaty the knob slipped out of my hand. I smelled Don's scent behind me. Finally opening the door I walked out but not before Don threw me onto the wall.

"Bitch you going to marry this nigga? What the fuck is wrong with you?!"

"Nothing is wrong with me! Get off of me before I tell Drew," I whispered.

"Tell him what bitch? How I made your ass cum on my fucking dick?! I thought you wasn't fucking him no more! So you just a lying ass bitch now?" he asked grabbing my neck. Before I knew it he had his hands between my thighs and grabbed onto my pussy. Moving my panties to the side, he rubbed onto my clit with his fingers. "You don't remember when I had you yelling out my name? Why you doing me like this? You see what you making me do? I knew something was up when you left last night and didn't return. You thought you were never going to return and leave me in the dust right? Well I was already two steps ahead of you plotting with your nigga," he said in my ear now inserting two fingers inside of me.

"Don please get off of me," I begged.

"Get off of you? You sure about that? Why you getting wet for daddy then?" he said sucking onto my neck. "Let me feel you ma," he said unbuckling his pants.

"No we can't," I told him pushing him. He put his hands up with a devious smirk plastered on his face. Rushing to my car, I slammed the door and drove off. If I mentioned anything about Don to Drew, I knew it my heart things would never be the same.

*****

"Wait, wait repeat yourself?" Sophia asked me once we finished ordering our drinks.

"I said, when I left the house Don was there," I repeated. We went to a place close to the hospital where Sophia worked at. The burgers were so good here! I was feening to have one. This place has been here for years and Sophia and I use to come here when we were younger. I had to explain to her what happened before I came to meet up with her, minus the ending.

That's not all, I finally had sex!" she screamed out in excitement. Once again the people inside the restaurant eyes looked in our direction. Downing my drink, I grabbed Sophia hand telling her it was time to go find somewhere else to go, ain't no telling if we have any other outburst in here.

"Bitch, you told me you been had sex," I whispered in her ear on the way out.

"Yeah, yeah I know. Look long story…"

Yeah, this was going to be a long night.

*****

Stumbling in the house after leaving the bar, I tripped on thin air. I knew I was fucked up and should've never mixed my drinks but I just couldn't stop myself. From laughing, crying and laughing some more with Sophia, I had the best time of my life. We had to take cabs home because we were too fucked up, me more than her.

"Where the fuck was you?" I heard Drew voice, but I couldn't see him. The sudden bright lights made my eyes squint.

"I told you I was out with Sophia," I responded taking off my boots.

"I've been calling you for the past few hours. Why weren't you answering? If we are going to get married, all this stops now. I'm trying to become better and--"

"I just got in the house! I don't want to hear this shit!" I said stumbling while taking off my other boot.

"I don't give a fuck! You need to slow down with all this damn drinking too! You're not a teenager anymore!"

"You know what? I don't have time for this!" Grabbing my sneakers from by the door, I put them on before I called me an uber to someone I knew would want to be around me. Getting in my uber, Drew was calling me but I ignored his call. *Fuck him with his uptight ass!*

Knock! Knock!

I could hear music blasting from inside the house, so I turned around and started kicking at the door. The loud music abruptly came to a stop, so my kicking antics must have worked. Once the door opened, I was greeted by a gun in my face.

"It's just me!" I screamed.

"Why the fuck are you kicking at my door twelve in the morning!" Don yelled, placing the gun down.

"Who you got in here?" I asked ignoring his question, brushing past him.

"Not you!" he responded following behind me.

"Oh this we doing now? I was just here yesterday!" I screamed pointing to a female he had sitting on his couch.

"Before or after you got engaged? You are tripping."

"Sorry boo but you got to go," I told the female. She rolled her eyes at me before she continued doing what she was doing. "I said you got to go!" I yelled again now walking in her direction.

"Don?" She called out as he shrugged his shoulders. "Nigga don't call me no more!" She yelled getting her stuff together.

"I didn't even call you, you called me," he said to her while she walked out the door.

"You fucked her?" I asked him.

"I was about to before you came and ruined shit," he said sitting back down. Grabbing some weed off the table, he put it inside of a blunt getting ready to roll it up. Going into his pocket, he pulled out a blue baggie with white substance in it. He must have felt my eyes on him because he looked up at me for a few seconds before opening the baggie and pouring whatever was in it, into the blunt.

"What are you doing?" I asked.

"What does it look like I'm doing?"

"What is that?"

"What does it look like?"

"Stop being an ass and asking me questions after I ask you one!"

"So stop asking stupid fucking questions," he responded sealing the blunt with his lips.

"Are you on drugs?" I asked in disbelief.

"Do I look like a drug addict?" he asked lighting the blunt.

"Well no, you don't. Do you do this often?"

"Nah not really, only when I need something a little stronger when people stress me the fuck out."

"Why are you stressed? I think you should stop doing this," I told him getting close to where he was seated on the couch.

"It ain't that serious ma, just to clear my head. And as for the stress, that's you stressing me out.

"How I'm stressing you?"

"Because you don't know what you want and I'm done with your little games. You making a nigga crazy just for your attention," he admitted.

"Your right, I don't know and yes I am sorry. I'm sorry for bringing you into this but you knew I had a man from the beginning." Taking another pull from the blunt, he grabbed my face, planted his lips onto mines, and blew the smoke into my mouth. I immediately blew the smoke out of my mouth.

"Why the hell would you do that after you just put that shit in there!" I yelled.

"Stop all that yelling shit and just try it," he said.

"No, I don't need that shit!"

"Where is the Melody that I first met? The one that was down to do anything? You act like we never smoked weed together and you crying over a little white dust! Man whatever!"

"It's not like that, people can get addicted to that stuff Don," I explained.

"Well do I look addicted? Exactly. You seem a little tense anyway, you need something to relax that ass!"

"I am not tense. Shut up and just pass it to me!" I yelled.

"That's my baby. You know I'll never do anything to hurt you," he said passing me the blunt. I put it to my lips and inhaled it. I didn't feel anything out of the ordinary so I decided to take an even longer pull. Passing the blunt back to Don he smiled and smoked it for a few more minutes.

"Wait, let me get another pull," I told him as he passed it to me again and I took two more pulls. Snatching it back from me, he told me I had enough and needed to relax because I was already intoxicated. I told him I was good and to not worry. Almost instantly, I started to feel the effects from the weed or coke, at this point I didn't know which one but it felt good, in a weird way. I felt my mouth getting wet and my heart beating through my chest. I wanted to talk but no words would come out. My vision was getting a little foggy and my body felt stuck to the couch. Next thing I knew, Don lips was on mines. I tried to tell him to stop but the different motion's that were taking over my body was too strong to fight.

"Shhh. You know I got you baby, just let me take care of you," he said kissing me on the lips again. Feeling him wrapping his arms around me, I felt secured.

Sophia

A few months later...

"Black you promised you was going to help me move into my apartment today!" I yelled to him over the phone... Me and Shay was at her new home while I waited for Black. Since dealing with Black, Shay and I grew a bond. At first, when he told me he had a female friend he was close to, I was a little iffy about it because of that Karma situation that happened back then. Being a man of his word with nothing to hide, he introduced me to Shay and I haven't felt a bad vibe from her yet. She was like the big sister I never had. Me and Melody was still close, but with what was going on with her and Don, things definitely did change. Before Black, I wasn't that experienced with relationships, but what I did know was, what she was doing was wrong.

"Yes baby I know, something came up though," he said over the facetime call.

"You said that last week!" Rolling my eyes, I stood the phone up on the counter.

"You look so sexy when you mad baby," he smiled showing off his pearly whites.

"Quintel, I'm not in the mood for your shit!"

"Ohh, she called you *Quintelll*!" Shay yelled in the background amping it.

"If you don't help me move in, somebody else would," I told him before hanging up.

"Now I don't know why you stay playing with his crazy ass," Shay laughed sitting on her Floral sofa eating crackers and cheese. I told her to not eat it all day because she was going to get constipated, but I learned you cannot tell a pregnant woman nothing.

"I'm just so ready to move into my new place, I just get jealous every time I come to your newly furnished home," I sadly replied.

"Girl trust me, if Black wanted to do it, he would've been did it. If I don't know anything about him, I know he makes time for whatever is a priority in his life."

"Why wouldn't him helping me move into my apartment be a priority?"

"Ummmm because he doesn't want you to move into your own place, duh," she laughed.

"Well it's already too late. What's the problem with having my own? I know he wants his own space and wasn't ready for a live in girlfriend and I understand that. Before it gets to that point, I want to remove myself from the situation overall." I stated.

"Hmph. Okay, whatever you feel is right but don't say I didn't warn you," she chuckled shaking her head and rubbing her belly. She was due to give birth very soon. She was so huge, you would've thought it was twins, but she was having a baby boy. Finally accepting that Black once again, wasn't going to come and help me do what I had to do, I decided to handle it myself, making an appointment with U-Haul to help me with all my things. I mainly had just clothes and stuff at Black's place, so that could stay there. It wasn't like I was not going to come and spend the night sometimes. Chilling and watching Netflix was me and Shay thing, we were currently watching a show called The Last O.G. Grabbing the pack of crackers off the table with a few slices of cheese, I felt Shay burning a hole in me with her eyes, most likely not wanting to share her goodies.

"Don't be a brat," I told her.

"I'm not being a brat," she lied rolling her eyes and pressing play.

Black

"Ew you stink," Shay cared to share after opening up the front door. I knew she was referring to me smelling like I bathed in liquor. A nigga just had a few drinks…. okay maybe more than a few, but I was good enough to drive over here, so I'm good.

"So do you. Where is she?" I asked referring to Sophia.

"She sleeps on the couch still. You come over here this time of night all drunk and shit. And yall better not fuck on my new couches, I didn't even break them in yet," she said wobbling to the stairs.

"Yeah aight," I responded walking into the living room. Sophia was knocked out, snoring lightly with a little quilt on top of her body. I sat and watched her for a little before I decided to go in the bathroom and brush my teeth since Shay said I stank and what not. I'm glad she had some extra unused toothbrushes down here, it definitely came in handy.

"Oh shit," I laughed to myself because I tripped and almost fell coming out of the bathroom. Finally reaching the couch Sophia was resting at, I bent down to her ear until my lips was touching them. "Who you going to get to help you move your shit?" I asked her. Still in the middle of sleeping it didn't register to her what was going on as she awakens. Rubbing her eyes, she looked confused to see me standing over her.

"When did you get here?" she asked looking around the living room.

"Who's going to help you move your shit?" I asked her sitting down next to her. She tried to get up but I pulled her closer to me.

"Obviously not you," rolling her eyes.

"Chill baby something came up," I told her putting my arm around her.

"What exactly came up? Huh? Going out and getting drunk doing who knows the fuck what?"

"Aye, you need to lower your tone before I give you a reason to be yelling. Nah it wasn't none of that, did you forget I had a meeting today?" I asked her. Dawning to her, what I was referring to, she looked me up and down intaking my wardrobe. I knew I was coming to talk business at the meeting, so that's how I was going to present myself. Instead of my usual gear, I was looking like I wanted to talk money with a royal blue tux with the matching pants. Unbuttoning the tux, I removed the bottom of my white button up from inside my pants. Putting her hand over her mouth she apologized about how she forgot.

"Oh baby, how did it go? You look so good, how did I not notice? I was so caught up with my shit I forgot. I feel so bad," she pouted.

"Nah you good. I know I have been telling you for a while I was going to handle that for you. Just give me some time aight? And about the meeting it went real well. It's a deal! Everything should go smoothly from here on out. I haven't met the nigga Vito yet, I had a one on one talk with Nas, they both co owners of the club. I have been on it with him since the day after I had that welcome home party at the club. That shit was tight, I just had to see the creator of it, and to come find out he was a black man motivated me even more," I excitedly exclaimed. I been into a lot of illegal shit in my life. Jail wasn't for me and I was never going back there so I had to think smart about the money moves I was going to be making.

"Baby I'm so proud of you." Holding my face gently she kissed me repeating how much she was proud of me.

"You so proud of your man huh? Show me how much," I told her unloosing my tie.

"Okay, let me go get my things so we can go," she said trying to get up.

"Nah baby I don't want to wait. You know ever since you let me inside of you, I can't get enough of you," I admitted. That shit Sophia had between her legs had me hooked. I haven't thought about sliding in shit else since then!

"No. What if Shay catches us?" she whispered as I lifted up her shirt to attack the most perfect breast I saw in my life.

"Didn't you say I can have it whenever I want it?" I asked her.

"Yes, but--"

"But nothing, you are about to get this shit and I was drinking Henny don't play with me girl. Tell me you want me. I want to know you want it baby," I pleaded. She had me out here sounding like Keith Sweat and shit.

"I want you baby, give it to me," she moaned caving in while I gave her breast some attention.

"Well not in here!" I heard Shay scream. Sophia hurried up and pulled her shirt down rising off the couch. Her cheeks flushed with embarrassment. We didn't even hear her approach us.

"Hating ass! Ain't you supposed to be sleep? Damn!" I told her grabbing Sophia hand.

"I got hungry," she responded.

"Come on baby, my car hot and ready for you," I joked walking towards the door.

"Goodnight Shay, Shay," Sophia called out.

"Yeah, yeah whatever," she said locking the door.

"You were serious about the car?" Sophia asked shyly. Shit, sometimes I forget I got to take certain shit slowly with her because I was her first so she wasn't use to a lot of shit.

"If you are not comfortable with it baby it's cool, I can wait until we get to my spot," I told her.

"No baby… It's okay… I kind of like the car idea," she said grabbing my dick from outside of my pants. *Damn, I think I created a freak.*

Melody

After wiping myself on the toilet, I noticed blood on the tissue. *Just great*, I thought. That must have been the reason why I woke up in pain. Don was getting on my damn nerves and I needed to get out of here. I had a few toiletries here, grabbing a pad from underneath the sink, I walked towards the door.

"I'm leaving!" I yelled to Don. *Don? How did I end up back here again?* I just remember drinking last night and arguing again with Drew. I was getting so disappointed in myself; this shit was like a pattern.

"You leaving? Where the fuck you going? You going back to that nigga? I dare you to say yeah so I can let him know was sup!" Don yelled coming towards me.

"Did I say that? Did I say I was going there? I just need some damn air okay!" I yelled back. All this bickering and arguing was becoming overbearing for me. Grabbing my wrist, he threw me into the wall.

"Who the fuck are you talking to like that?" he calmly ask. Too calm if you asked me, this man was turning insane. How did I miss the signs from the beginning?

"You don't have to hit me!"

"I didn't hit your ass yet!" he yelled.

"Please, please, I just need some air," I begged getting light headed. Before I knew it, I was holding my mouth running to the bathroom. This stress was taking a big toll on me, mentally and physically. Throwing up the sandwich I just ate, I felt disgusted.

"Why the hell you throwing up?" Don asked sincerely. See crazy? This man was bipolar.

"I don't knowwww," I whined between gags.

"How much did you take today?" he asked.

"How much of what?" I responded. Flushing the toilet, I went to the sink to wipe my mouth.

"You want to act stupid? Don't make me ask you again."

"I didn't take a lot Don!," I lied. I was high as a kite, that's why I had these damn shades on. I was trying to get out before he saw me and start nagging me about it. He's the one who gave me the coke in the first place and now have something to say every time I needed a little extra boost.

"You didn't take a lot but you're here throwing up? Why the hell you got on shades for in the house?" he asked grabbing them off my face with so much force, I wouldn't be surprised if they were broken.

"Look at you! You look fucking stupid! High as shit you idiot. What I told you about going into my shit? So what you telling me your an addict now? I don't fuck with bitches addicted to drugs," he said rolling his eyes.

"But it's your drugs!" I yelled feeling tears form in my eyes.

"Say that shit any louder and watch what happens to you," he said, sitting on the couch.

"I hate you! Look what you did to me! It's all your fucking fault," I screamed. Oh, I wasn't done with his ass yet!

"It's my fault that you got bored with your relationship and started to look for new dick to entertain you? So you're telling me that all because of me? I didn't force you to do fucking nothing! Everything was willingly. Just like you willingly gave up that worn out ass pussy!" he laughed evilly. Feeling like I had all the strength in the world, I ran and jumped on top of him on the couch clawing at his face. "Stupid. Bitch..." I heard him scream out before I was thrown onto the floor. Getting on top of me, he slapped me so hard, my vision blurred. "Now you can go!" he screamed and that's exactly what I did. It seems like I won't be here for a while, I'm glad something told me to steal his stash. Another reason why I was trying to leave so fast.

Walking to my car, I grabbed my phone going straight to Drew's name. *Shit, I can't call him.* Having no other option, I called Melody.

"Hey girl," she answered out of breathe.

"What's wrong your busy?" I asked.

"Yeah, I'm here at my new place trying to put all this stuff away. I came over to your house a few days ago to pack up all my things. Where were you?" she asked.

"Oh, umm…. probably out shopping," I lied, knowing damn well I was with the devil himself, Don.

"Wait, something happened between you and my brother?" I asked.

"No, none of that. I just wanted my own space you know. By the way, if you see him don't tell him," she responded.

"Whatever that means, send me the location, I'm about to come over," I told her.

Sending me the location, I put in my GPS system. I would've gotten there in ten minutes, but I dragged time before she questioned how I arrived so fast. Also, I was trying to wait until this high wear down some more. I drove around drinking milk, I didn't know if it would work or not but I read it up on google. After finally letting her know I was outside her apartment, she gave me the bell number. Thankfully Don didn't break my shades, so I still had those to cover my eyes if I wasn't looking like myself.

When I got to the front of her apartment door, we embraced one another with a much needed hug, well on my behalf. "Wow, I missed my friend," I told her breaking down in her arms. So much was going on in my life, and I blame myself for pushing everybody away. Who even knows the last time I spoke to my mother. I was embarrassed for all the actions that I was making. Sophia rubbed my back ensuring me everything was going to be okay. She didn't know half of the things I was going through, but at least somebody still had hope for me.

"I'm over at Melody's house," Sophia lied on the phone to Black. He called her shortly after I reached her new apartment. Everything wasn't intact but it was starting off real good.

"Oh word? Aight I'm about to come over there," he responded.

"No it's okay, I'll be over soon, if not I'll stay the night. I didn't see my best friend in a while, you know?"

"Aight, I understand, I'm about to go handle something so I'm going to call you back," he said hanging up.

"Why don't you just tell him you moved into your own place?" I asked confused.

"Because he didn't want to help me move into here in the first damn place!" she said making the plates. Not really the one to make five course meals, Sophia made spaghetti and garlic bread. Hell, I wasn't complaining because my stomach was starting to hurt from hunger. The last thing I ate, I threw up, I was definitely hungry.

"Well, you wouldn't be able to hide it for long, so we'll see," I responded grabbing the plate out of Sophia hands. The spaghetti just came out of the pot, but the heat was the least of my worries. I devoured my food, without even taking a break to breathe.

"Well damn. Somebody was hungry," Sophia laughed blowing the spaghetti that was wrapped around her fork to cool down. "Are you dieting? It looks like you lost weight." I was in the kitchen on my way to the pot to make seconds.

"Really?" I asked looking down at myself. "Oh... Umm... I started doing that keto diet you told me about awhile back," I lied. From the stress and the drugs, who knows what the cause of my weight lost was.

"I'm pretty sure on keto, you can't eat pasta, and on top of that, bread."

"Everybody deserves a cheat day," I laughed trying to blow her off.

"Okay, just don't lose too much, your weight always looked good on you."

"I'll try not to," I responded.

Sitting down on the couch, my phone started to ring, getting both of our attentions. *Don*, the screen read. We both looked up at one another at the same time. Laying back on the couch, I started my second round of spaghetti.

"So you're not going to answer?" she questioned.

"Nah, it's not that important," I responded to her cutting the conversation short. Otherwise, hanging with Sophia, I had no worries going through my head. Drew nor Don knew where I was at, so my head wasn't so crowded with what ifs. It felt good to be around somebody who just accepted me for me.

Waking up, I realized me and Sophia fell asleep on the couch watching her television that wasn't on the stand yet, instead it was on the floor. Slowly rising off the couch, making sure not to wake her, I tiptoed to my bag to have my every night fixed, well everyday but who's counting. What started out as a little boost to put in the weed turned into something more. I wasn't big on smoking weed, but I liked the high I got from the coke so Don thought it would be a good idea if I was to just sniff it instead. He was tired of me getting my lip gloss on the blunt anyway. Maybe it can help me get rid of these damn cramps too. Limping to the bathroom, I turned on the light. Sitting my bag on the sink, I grabbed the bag of drugs and sat on the toilet with it. Taking some out, I placed it on the side of the sink and adjusted my body so I could lean over and sniff it. Before I can get any closer, I felt a sharp pain in my lower back.

"Fuck!" I called out, leaning back up I rubbed my lower back where the pain was coming from. I suddenly started to feel a little light headed. Pulling down my pants, I lifted the toilet seat holding the side of the bathroom sink in extraordinary pain.

"Ouchhh!" I screamed out in pain. My body started to feel like it was overheating. Rocking back and forth, I felt the pain getting worse. *Please god make it stop*, I silently prayed in my head. Looking down onto my pad, I realized it was more blood than usual on there for my first day. At this point, my back was aching, my body was overheating and I felt like I was going to pass out.

"Sophiaaa!" I called out in need of help. *'Please help me"*, I whispered holding onto my belly rocking back and forth. Opening the bathroom door a few seconds later looking out of it, she asked me what was wrong looking at me confused, before she could see the drugs, I tried to knock it onto the floor but it was already too late.

"What the fuck is that? Melody what is going on?" Sophia asked panicking.

"It's nothing, please help me in so much painnnn," I cried.

"Pain, why? Is it because of that? What is that?" she asked again running to my side sitting on the edge of the tub.

"I have bad cramps, I thought maybe a little would help," I tried to lie, hoping she would believe me. Well it technically wasn't a lie.

"So you thought this drug would help with cramps? What is it, please you probably can die, I need to know, you know I am a nurse," Sophia cried.

"I'm not going to die, it's only coke," I forced out, trying to catch my breath.

"Only COKE?!" she screamed.

"Please I need you, my stomach, I'm in so much pain, call the ambulance ... wait no, they may find it in my system," I cried. I didn't want to be labeled as a drug addict. Grabbing her hand, I felt like I had to shit, so I pushed and pushed until I felt gust of relief come over me. "Wait, no don't call them, I think... I think... I think I feel a little better now." Getting off the toilet, I pulled my pants back up. Before I could flush the toilet, I saw something strange inside of it. Before I could comment about how big the blood clot looked, Sophia beat me to it.

"What the fuck is that? Did you just have a miscarriage in my bathroom? You were pregnant?" She asked holding her mouth.

"Not that I knew of, I'm going to hell, I killed my baby," I cried breaking down.

"Did Drew know?" she asked sincerely.

"I don't even know if the baby was his," I cried even louder. Sophia looked at me with pity as I cried on her shoulder. I think I officially reached my lowest point.

"We have to go to the hospital, like now," she responded putting the back of her hand on my forehead to check my temperature.

*****

Sophia drove me to the hospital that she worked out. Being that she was an employee and this was an emergency, I didn't have to wait long. I immediately got admitted and the nurse started to work on me. Taking my vitals, blood, and everything else. She asked me when my last period was and I didn't even remember. *How could I be pregnant and not even know?* I was confused and the pain was starting to return as I laid down on the bed, with a curtain separating me and the other patients. I'm glad during this time, Sophia didn't bring up what she saw in the bathroom, but I knew that wouldn't be for long. After waiting in silence for about thirty minutes, a nurse came inside. She asked Sophia to step out of the room, but I assured her that it was fine.

"Okay. Hello, my name is Nurse Samuel and I'll be your nurse for the night. So, Ms. Love according to your HCG levels, you were indeed pregnant. Considering that you had a miscarriage which can cause the levels to drop so we wouldn't indeed have an exact time frame of how far you were. Taking a guess, I would say two months, but you could've been further.

The sono tech will come shortly to check you and make sure everything happened smoothly..." The more the nurse talked, the more I started to space out. *Pregnant?* This is my first time ever pregnant because I'm very big on birth control. Too much was going on in my life, I haven't even though of a birth control pill in months. Drew and I haven't been having sex a lot but it still can be a possibility that the baby was his. But, with my luck, I knew this baby was no others than Don's.

After everything was done and they sent me on my way, I was debating between going home or just staying with Melody. I just wanted to come clean about everything and let go, but I was scared of what his reaction would be. I thought I wanted out, but I cannot picture my life without Drew. As if Sophia was reading my mind, she asked me where I was staying at, I told her to just drop me off at her place. Trying to get out the car, the child proof locks was on.

"I won't judge you because I love you. I don't understand how this happened, or what's going on in your life to make you turn to drugs, but I am here for you. If you stop right now, we never have to talk about it again, I won't tell anybody. Just promise me you'll get it together, I am here you," Sophia sadly spoke while tears slowly came down her face.

"I promise, I'm done," I told her, or at least I thought so.

Karma

"I'm about to be out," Nino told me getting up.

"Why? Where are you going?" I asked him wrapping the sheet around me.

"To go meet up with Black--," before he could finish, I cut him off.

"Can I come?" I asked as soon as I heard Black's name.

I been dealing with Nino on and off for the past few months. Well I wouldn't say dealing, I would say fucking. He's a close friend of Black's so I did feel bad. I don't think Black knows about this because he would've said something about it. Nino just had that dick you just had to keep coming back to. He was cool too, so it wasn't no biggie. He was the average size guy, but his sexiness took up for that. He had long braids that he kept straight to the back or coming down like ASAP rocky. He wasn't as dark as Black, but he would still be considered brown skinned. His skin was a perfect match to Haagen Dasz chocolate ice cream. His slim was built, but he had that 'don't fuck me with aura' so you knew he wasn't nothing to play with. His bedroom eyes also gave him, his sex appeal.

"Why?" he questioned sitting up on the bed fasten his construction boots.

"We never hang out, you just come over for sex and then you leave. Pleaseeee, I don't have any plans tonight and I don't want to be cooped up in the house alone."

"So call somebody over."

"No! What's the problem? Why can't I come out with you? Because Black is going to be there?"

"Shawty, now are you tripping. Fuck I'm worried about you around my mans? You ain't my girl," he responded shaking his head.

"Exactly, so are why you acting like it's a problem?"

"You know what, get dressed and I'm not driving your ass back home. Hurry up with your nagging ass!" I rushed off the bed jumping up and down with excitement on the inside. Ha! I couldn't wait to see the look on Blacks face when he sees me with his homeboy.

After my quick shower, I made sure to put on some fly sexy shit so Black couldn't help but notice me. I didn't know if we were going to a club, a restaurant, or even to chill on the block. It didn't matter to me. I was coming to step out tonight. I had on a blue tight satin dress with a twist in the front and also open sleeve with some gold pointy heels that went perfect with it. My hair was in a bob cut with a Chinese bang in the front. I was definitely going to turn multiple heads tonight. Applying my light makeup on, I was ready to go.

We arrived at the same club, Blackout that Black had his welcome home party at. I have been here a few times so it wouldn't be a new experience. I tried to grab Nino's arm but he looked at me like I was crazy. "You got one more time to do some dumb shit like we a couple or something," he said walking ahead of me as I followed. *Maybe I'll just have to make Black jealous another way.* Following Nino to a section with a few people I've never seen before. I don't think he arrived yet, which was good. I still had time to come up with an idea. I saw his little sister Melody and waved to her, she rolled her eyes at me and turned her head. *Well fuck you too.*

"Why is she here?" She asked loudly enough making everyone turn their heads in my direction. Nino shrugged his shoulders and laughed. I poured me a shot and ignored them all. If somebody wanted me to leave, they better make me leave or else I'm staying right here waiting…

"Black!" Before I could get my thoughts together, I heard somebody yelling out his name. Looking at the entrance of the section, I stared hard waiting for him to notice me. I got up to walk to him, when I felt myself getting yanked back down.

"Don't even try it." Turning around, it was Black little sister with the mean grill. Rolling my eyes I turned my head back around to see him entering the section with….

"Hey everybody," she said smiling. *The dyke? Wait a minute, this is the same girl I saw leaving out his place! So he been fucking with her all these years? No it can't be….*

He pulled her in front of him so she can move in first. *When did Black become a gentleman?* She had on a white strapless Zion dress. Little specks of glitter glistened on her chest each time a light reflected on her along with the diamond tennis chain on her neck. The freckles surrounding her face made her look exotic. Walking more inside the section, with Black holding her from the back, the smiles on their faces made me angry with envy flowing through my veins. Scanning everybody in the room, she looked at me with a surprised look. I smiled and waved while she turned to whisper in Black's ear, pointing in my direction. He looked at me next and then whispered something into her ear before replacing his words with his tongue and grabbing on her ass. *Really?* She walked past me and sat next to Melody. Just before I was about to pour me another shot, I was yanked up.

"Time to go," Black told me pulling me in the direction of the entrance of the section.

"Why do I got leave to leave? Is it because I came here with Nino? Are you jealous?" I pressed.

"Jealous of what? That yall fucking?" he asked.

"How do you know that?"

"Because I told him he could," he said laughing, turning around to go about his business.

I was floored. He told him he could fuck me? What kind of fucking games were being played? Now he was making me seem fucking delusional. Fuck Black and everybody he's acquainted with! He was making me hate him. Realizing I didn't have a ride either got me so fucking fed. Going through the back door of the club because it was closer, I heard a man on the phone.

"Yeah, that coked out bitch in there parading that nigga Drew in her arms like she just wasn't just sucking my dick. What?... Yeah that nigga Drew that be with Black…. Oh word? He just came home though you think he still got money like that?... Shit, I think we just found our next come up…Aight bet, bet, I'm going to holla at you later." The mysterious guy hung up the phone and bumped right into me.

"The fuck you looking at?" he asked.

"Something that I like," I responded, quick on my toes.

"Oh word? You look like something that I might consider liking too. What's your name?" he asked.

"My name Karma, what's your name? Daddy," I flirted.

"Nah my shit Don, but you can call me daddy. Here take my number down, I got shit to do but might need to slide in something warm and wet tonight after," he said reading me off his number.

Now I believe everything happens for a reason, Black could not deny my loyalty after this.

Sophia

"Don't let something like that happen again," I told Black.

"Baby, you know I would never. Look at you, bossing up and shit. You been around Shay crazy ass for too long now," Black laughed. I couldn't believe Karma had the audacity to show her face here, and with Nino at that. So she was just loving the crew? Girl was delusional. I thought that would be the craziest part of the night, not until I saw Don come sit in the section. So Drew was still hanging out with him? Once Melody told me how the drug intake started, it made me hate Don even more. I wanted to come clean to Black about it so bad, but I was stuck between a rock and a hard place. If I told him, I knew Melody would be upset and feel like I went against her. I was already involved from lying from the beginning saying that he was my cousin. If I knew it would've went this far, I would have never agreed in the first place. I hope this is the furthest it would get, but in the back of my mind, I knew this was only the beginning.

"Come baby, I would like for you to meet somebody." Black whispered in my ear. Following his lead I stood up as a couple approached us. "Baby this is Nas, the man that I'm going to be working with for now on. Getting this club business popping and shit, feel me?" I gave him a handshake introducing myself with a smile. He was a handsome guy and you could tell he was about his business. Closely behind him was a brown skinned beauty. "And this is his wife Candy," Black continued. She was so beautiful, I couldn't believe it. Putting my arm out to also give her a handshake she looked down at my hand with a screwed up face.

"Uh-uh. We family now girl, we give hugs," she laughed bringing me in for a hug.

"Alright Candy, before you scare the girl. She might think you coming onto her," Nas joked.

"Don't be jealous," she laughed.

"But word, welcome to the family yall. Now let's get this money!" Nas said. Him and Black embraced into a brotherly hug. I was really proud of Black trying to turn his life around for the better. This is just what he needed. Excusing myself, I walked over to Melody who had a worried look on her face.

"What happened?" I asked her. Not even replying, she unlocked her phone to show me her and Don messages. Attached was a video. Pressing play, I gasped in shock to see Melody giving, who I'm guessing, Don oral sex. Not only that, white powdery substance was all over her face in the video. Looking up, Don eyes was on us. He blew Melody a kiss, glancing around quickly, I made sure nobody noticed.

"What am I going to do? He's threatened to send it to Drew. Sophia you have to help me, I don't want Drew to leave me. I promise I haven't been using or been with Don ever since that day I lost the baby. Please help me, what am I going to do?" she cried. Feeling bold, Don walked over to us, sitting directly next to Melody.

"So what's its going to be?" he asked Melody.

"Please not here," she begged.

"Time is ticking, but I'm sure you will make the right decision. This should teach you a fucking lesson about playing with people feelings. Enjoy your night," he said getting up and walking out of the section.

"You have to help me come up with something, please," she begged.

"I'll try, I'll try okay," I responded.

"What was that all about?" Black asked walking up to us.

"Nothing, he was looking for Drew," Melody lied.

"What side of your family you said he was from again?" Black asked suspiciously.

"Yo Black come over here! I got some other people I need you to meet," Nas said, calling Black over.

Turning my head, before I could speak on what just happened, Melody beat me to it. "I know, I know. Please just give me some time. I'm going to figure this all out and Don would be just a memory. Please?" she begged. I hope like hell none of this interfered with my relationship.

Melody

Today was a day I was dreading, going to see my mother. I purposely ignored her for months. A mother knows their child and I just wasn't ready to admit any of my wrong doings. Pulling up the front of the house, I stared at what used to be my old home, when life was good, nothing like I was going through now. If I could just rewind back time, I would in a heartbeat. Stepping out of the car, I slowly walked to the front of the door. Trying to keep it all together, before I could knock, the door flew open.

"Hi mommy," I lowly spoke in a childlike voice.

"Oh my baby, it's okay, everything is going to be okay," she said, hugging me while I broke down in her arms. *Everybody was telling me over and over that everything was going to be okay, but was it really?*

Walking inside the house, that I haven't visited in months, I felt safe. Secured. Sitting on the chair, I braced myself to let everything out that I've been going through for the past few months. "Drew has been very worried about you. He came over here a few times," My mom informed me.

"Has he really?" I asked.

"Yes, what is going on with you Melody?"

"Mommy I messed up," I cried again, just silently this time.

"Who is he?" she asked already knowing it was dealing with a man.

"A guy I met, at first I didn't have any bad intentions I swear. He just made me feel….. made me feel like a woman again. All the affection and attention I was receiving from him made my cloudy days, sunny. I just needed a friend, but then things turned for the worst." I nervously played with my fingers. My right leg would not stop twitching no matter how much I tried to get it to stop. Anxiety took over my body. Never wanting to admit to your parents, even to someone that you love that you done drugs. "I let the feeling he gave me get to my head. It felt so right, even though I knew it was wrong. I was just lonely. I… I thought I didn't want to be with Drew anymore but it was a mistake. I started sleeping with this man. He… he gave me drugs and--"

"Drugs?!" she yelled.

"Please don't judge me, I've been clean ever since I lost the baby."

"BABY?!" she screamed.

"Mommy please. I need help. He's going to tell Drew, I'm scared. I messed up, I don't want to lose him. Everything is getting better and we're working on making us better." I cried.

"Who is this man? How does he know Drew? Is it a friend of his? Melody you have to fix this, you have to be honest," The wrinkles on her forehead formed quickly.

"You think he's going to leave me I'm scared?" I asked.

"Baby, the only way you would know and to get this off your shoulders is by telling the truth. I know you don't want to live your life in a lie anymore.

Ding!

Looking at my phone, I read the worst text of my life. I wasn't ready, I needed more time. My heart felt like it was ripped out of my chest. I never thought I would see this day coming. As much as I thought I wanted it, I was wrong.

DREW: *You don't got to worry anymore.*

Checking my call log, the last call was an outgoing call to Drew for the last ten minutes. He heard everything, he heard it all……..

Black

KARMA: *When you get a chance, hit me, it's important.*

    This girl was becoming a thorn in my spine. Ignoring her text, I pulled up in front of Sophia new apartment. She thought she was so damn slick. I'm the one who showed her the place from the beginning. Just to get her to shut up because she was just so fiend out to get a place. What I didn't mention to her, and I'm glad I didn't was that I owned the building. I never dealt with a woman that didn't want me to take care of them, so this was different for me. It turned me on, no lie, but Sophia don't understand that she's mine, so all that is out the window. I take care of what belongs to me. On the low, I wanted to see what she was doing behind a nigga back too. The doorman confirmed she didn't have no niggas in here coming to see her. Which she better not had. The way I felt five years ago was ten times worse now. Before I could control it, but no lie, she had a nigga all the way open now. Taking my key out, I made my way inside her apartment to get comfortable. I been here a few times, but this time she was going to notice my present. Going inside the fridge, it wasn't really shit inside because shorty stayed at my crib most of the time, which is why this apartment was pointless! I made me a sandwich and turned on the television until Sophia arrived. Most likely within an hour. I was clocking her and usually she come here before coming to my crib.

DREW: *Yo, we got to talk. Hit my line ASAP.*

Before I could call him, I heard the front door unlocking. *Shit!* She was earlier than usual. Going inside her room, I ran into her closet. Stuffing my face with the sandwich I just made. *Buzz! Buzz!* My phone started to vibrate inside my pocket. Taking it out, Sophia was calling me.

"Hey babe, where are you? I just came from your place and you're not there, so I stopped by to come see my mother. Check your phone, I am sending you a text now," she said leaving a voicemail.

SOPH: *I'm horny baby.*

Laughing on the inside, oh that's why it was urgent for her to know where I was, so I decided to just fuck with her.

ME: *I can't talk on the phone right now I'm in a meeting. Word? Show me.*

Sitting down onto her bed, she replied to me.

SOPH: *Show you? Show you how? On facetime? I thought you were in a meeting.*

ME: *Nah, send me a video of you playing with my pussy.*

SOPH: *Omg! Qutinel, no!*

ME: *Why not?*

SOPH: *I'm scared. LOL. Just hurry up.*

ME: *Please baby, you got me wanting it now. So you want to face time me? Ima mute the phone and just watch you okay. I want to see you. It would really make my day. I'm having a stressful ass day.*

I lied, I ain't do shit today, that's why I had enough free time to make my way over here. She stared at the phone, debating on what her next text should be so I sent another one over.

ME: *Please baby.*

SOPH: *Okay, okay…. give me a minute.*

Standing up, she took off each particle of clothing one by one. Getting on the bed, her back faced the headboard. She looked nervous as shit. She turned on the lamp on the dresser near her bed to give her some light because her room was dark, another reason why she wasn't able to see me. Grabbing her phone, she called me.

"Hey baby," she said into the phone. I had the phone low so she wouldn't be able to hear her voice. I nodded my head so she could continue. Taking the phone from in front of her face, I now had a clear view of her pussy. She slowly started to rub on it, still a little nervous. Pausing the facetime, I texted her again.

ME: *Just act like I'm there baby, act like it's me. You know how I make that pussy cum right? I want you to imagine that. Don't be shy, do this for Daddy.*

After reading the text, she smiled into the phone, telling me okay. Getting back into action, she wet her fingers with her mouth and proceeding to finish pleasing herself. Closing her eyes, she rubbed on herself in circular motions. Light moans escaped from her mouth. "Oh, Black," she moaned. I felt myself getting turned on from the show she was putting on. "Please hurry baby, I need you," she said. Little did she know, I was already here but I was enjoying the show, so I was going to let a little more time go by. She stopped rubbing and placed two fingers inside of her, fucking herself. "I wish this was your dick inside of me instead baby," she moaned moving her fingers faster. Her breathing started to speed up and I knew she was on the verge of releasing. I licked my lips, wishing it was me to be providing her the pleasure. My dick felt like it was about to break.

"Black, I'm cuminggg," she moaned, her eyes were closed shut, so she didn't see me come from inside the closet. Getting on the bed, her eyes opened in shock, before she could speak. I grabbed her legs forcing them open, placing myself inside its happy place.

"You overstayed your welcome, it's time to come where you belong, with me," I told her stroking inside of her.

"Okay baby," she moaned.

Shit, that was easy.

Melody

They said the truth will set you free right? Well that was a damn lie! Drew left me and I didn't have to think twice about that. I went home after receiving that text and he was gone. Nothing was out of place but I knew in my heart my relationship was over. I found my way to a bar, drinking my sorrows away. Shot after shot, my problems I was facing was now becoming a distant memory. The liquor was giving my courage... Courage, to face everything. *Fuck Don! He was a drug addict anyway! Fuck Drew! Maybe he should've paid more attention to me! No, I mean I miss him.*

"Ughhh!" I screamed out in frustrating.

"Stop making all that noise and let's go," I heard a voice from behind me request. Turning around, I noticed it was Nino, Black's friend. "You need to get out of here," he told me, taking a seat next to me by the bar.

"Boy, I am grown, please," I told him. "Why are you even here, I never saw you here before."

"That's irrelevant," he told me.

"Oh, so I guess you heard about what happened. Are you here to judge me? I don't do drugs anymore. The cheating was a mistake. Matter fact, I don't even care. Think what you want to think."

"I didn't know about all of that, that's your business, not mine. Your brother is worried about you, so let's go."

"NO! I don't have to leave if I don't want to. What? You came to rescue the day or something? Let me be!" I yelled.

"What I'm not going to do is chase you and beg you. You want to stay here? Aight, cool. He'll just have to come and get your ass himself. I got shit to do anyway. *Little ass girl*," I heard him mumble walking away. I was going to reply back to him, but he wasn't even worth it. I'll get in his ass later about that. Looking down at my phone, Sophia was calling me.

"Yeah?" I answered the phone.

"Why didn't you leave with Nino?" she asked.

"Word travel fast around these parts, isn't that right?" I asked her.

"What is that supposed to mean?"

"I guess when my brother started dicking you down, your loyalty to me went out the window?" I asked.

"Melody, what are you talking about?"

"I SAID it clear enough for you. What don't you understand? I asked you over and over to not say anything. As my FRIEND, I thought you wouldn't say shit to my brother, like I asked you. The dick is that good, huh?"

"First of all… you know what forget--"

"No, you got something to say? Get it off your chest, you have no other problems speaking about other shit!"

"You know what, your right? You think everything resolves fucking around you! You need to get your priorities fucking together! Okay! This whole fiasco you been doing, juggling around two men, and who knows what the fuck else. I haven't been anything but there for you, as you went ahead and made these stupid decisions. Instead of trying to work it out with your man, you thought it would be a good idea to start *riding* another man. Not only have I been keeping your stupid secrets, putting my relationship on the line, I never once judged you. And for the record, I didn't tell Black SHIT, Drew came over and I overheard the conversation that I soon have to explain. Grow the fuck up sometimes!" Sophia yelled and hung up the phone. *Well fuck her too! Let me get out of here before Black come looking for me.* Leaving a tip at the bar, I walked towards the door of the bar. It was now pitch black outside, I didn't even notice I was here for that long. I was intoxicated, but good enough to drive.

"Leaving so soon?" Suddenly stopping in my tracks, I turned around to see Don with a crazy look in his eyes. "Come here let me talk to you?"

"Please get away from me!" I yelled. Walking up to me, he grabbed my wrist and pulled me with so much force, it felt like my shoulder separated from the socket. "What the hell Don? Get off of me!"

"No! You are going to listen to me and what the hell I am about to say! Get in the car before I make a scene."

"No, I just want to go home. You ruined my life enough! Just stay away from me, before I call the cops."

"Call the cops? Bitch, I will kill you! I ruined your life? Start taking responsibility for your own actions! Now get in the car." He told me.

"I don't think you want to do that." It was as if God was answering my prayers because Nino appeared out of thin air. I thought he left.

"Don't worry about what the fuck is going on! This is my bitch, so my situation, keep the fuck on going, instead of trying to play save a hoe."

"Nah, this is my business. Yo Melody get up and let's go. If he was going to do anything. he would've done it by now," Nino replied, obviously upset.

Looking at Don, he stared at me with an expression that said 'bitch I dare you'. It was no way in hell I was going anyway with Don, so I made my way closer to Nino, closer to safety. Don was not having it though, "Bitch that's who you fucking now? How many niggas are you out here actually fucking? You sit there and cry about Drew bitch ass. I'm thinking I'm the next runner up and you were playing me too? You think this shit is a game right? Let me show you how funny it really is. If he dies, his blood is on your hands," Don said pulling his gun out of his waistband.

"Noo," I screamed, but it was already too late. He shot Nino in the chest before running to a car driving off. Taking off my shirt, I put pressure on the wound and prayed silently. "Please help! Call 9-1-1! Please," I cried. Nino eyes were now shut, I prayed he would make it. I don't know how I can live with this guilt of him dying, trying to protect me.

Karma

"Oh my god, what did you do?" I yelled, this was going too far now. This was not a part of the plan.

"The bitch been playing me this whole time," Don laughs as if he just didn't shoot somebody.

"Take Me Home, please," I begged.

"Take you home? After what you just saw, nah your ass staying right with me, and shut up that crying up! People get shot every day."

"Please don't kill me, I'm sorry. I promise I won't say anything."

"When I get my fucking money, I will decide on what I feel like doing with you."

I should've just left it alone. If Black didn't want me, I should've just accepted it. I already took away his freedom for four years, four years that he couldn't get back. Maybe this was my karma. *Please god get me out of this.* The plan that me and Don came up with, well more on his behalf, sounded like the perfect way to get back into Black's good graces. Don was supposed to kidnap Black's little sister, Melody, for a ransom. I told him I overheard him talking about Black at the club and wanted in. I spoke on Melody and how much I hated her. Also, I brought up Black also. I fed Don a lie about how Black was so in love with me and some more make believe shit. It took a little getting on his good side so that he could see I was serious about this. Once Don got the money from Black, that's when I was supposed to come and save the day and 'help' get Melody back to Black. He would always love me for returning his little spoiled sister back to him safely. But, this plan took a turn for the worst.

"Where are you taking me?"

"Somewhere far from here, we need to come up with another plan to get my money!"

"Don't you think it's too late for that! You just killed a man!"

"Good, now Black would know how serious I am. I just need to find a way to get into Melody's head." *This man is crazy!*

"But, you said nobody would get hurt," I cried.

"Well he should've never tried to come and play save-a-hoe. Shut the fuck up with all that shit before you get hurt next! You sitting here with tears and snot all over your face like you knew the nigga!"

Silence....

Turning around to face me, Don pulled the car over. "You knew that nigga? You were trying to set me up?" He asked placing his gun calmly on his lap.

"Yes, I know him... I mean no..." I lied. I didn't know to tell the truth or lie. My life was on the line and I know I did so fucked up shit, but I didn't want to die. Picking up the gun, he placed the metal steal on my temple.

"Yes or no? You got five seconds." My words were stuck in between my throat. I didn't know what to say or do. "Five….. Four….."

"Please Don. I don't know him like that," I lied. Of course I knew Nino; he was in my bed multiple times! "He's from around the way! Everybody knows him! It's impossible not to. He's like a hood celebrity. Please don't kill me… I don't want to die," I cried.

"You better hope I don't find out no shit." Don placed the gun back in his waist and started the car back up.

Karma was a bitch.

Sophia

I never went off on Melody like that but she really sparked a nerve. I couldn't believe she had the audacity to come at me like that. If I held her secret in for that long, why would she think I'll let it all out now? Not once, did she even consider that Drew actually told Black. She's been calling me for the last five minutes and I honestly didn't feel like talking to me. She never thinks about the decisions she makes before it goes too far.

"Sophia if you don't answer the damn phone already," Black groggily said. The noise from the phone ringing back to back must of woke him up.

"Melody I'm trying to get some sleep," I told her with an attitude.

"He... he shot him," she cried.

"What? Are you still at the bar? They were in there shooting? Where are you now?" My attitude immediately changed. The change in my tone and the words that were spoken out of my mouth caught Black's attention. I felt his eyes staring at me trying to get answers. I put Melody on speaker, not wanting to repeat anything she was saying, scared of what might come out of her mouth next.

"Don shot him right in front of me…"

"Don shot Drew?!" I asked in shock.

"No, he shot Nino!"

"Nino?" Black asked confused.

"I think he's dead. It's all my fault, I should've left when he told me too. Please come to the hospital. It's blood all over me. I am so scared Sophia," she cried into the phone. Black was already up and out the bed putting on his things when he heard it was Nino that got shot.

"Stay on the phone with me Melody, we are on our way. It's going to be okay…" I told her it was going to be okay, but I wasn't really sure. We got in the car, as Black sped through traffic, running lights, almost running bystanders over. Black and Nino were really close so I knew his mind was going crazy.

"Don…." He said to himself, putting his finger under his chin thinking about where he knew that name from. "Don… who the fuck is Don?!" Before I could speak, he turned to look at me. "Your fucking cousin shot Nino?!" He yelled. "Bet." Was all he said because focusing back on the road.

"Babe, wait... I have something to tell you." I knew this day was going to come, just not so soon and with somebody life on the line.

"Yo, Imma be real with you, that man is a dead man walking. If what you got to say is about that nigga save it, because I don't give a fuck," he said jumping out of the car and running into the hospital. I forgot Melody was even on the phone and if she heard anything, she knew her secret was about to come out, looking down, surprisingly she hung up. Following him, we made our way to the front desk so he could get information about where Nino was. The clerk informed him we had to go to the second floor and Nino's status was unknown. Sweat dripped down Black's face. I never saw him this nervous before.

"Baby, everything is going to be okay," I said, trying to console him. Reaching the second floor, we saw Melody with her hands covering her face, crying silently. Blood was all over her clothing. Her right leg was shaking uncontrollably. Looking up, she saw Black and I walking towards her.

"Black I'm so sorry," she cried.

"You ain't got shit to be sorry about," he told her sitting down. "What did they say about Nino? What the fuck is going on? They weren't trying to tell me shit at the desk," he asked obviously in an emotional state. His voice broke down even more with each word he spoke. Melody shook her head not watching to speak. "Yo Melody you got to tell me something! Niggas have to pay for this!" he yelled.

"He flatlined in the ambulance, that's all I know. I've been sitting here ever since. Everything is my fault," Melody said breaking down again.

"How the fuck is it your fault?" Black asked obviously upset.

Before Sophia could admit her wrong doings, a doctor came walking in our direction. Looking at all the blood on Melody clothing, the doctor knew we were here for the gunshot victim. "The family of Antonino Simmons?"

"Yeah that's me," Black stood up and said.

"Hello, I am Doctor Bruce and I apologize about what happened to Antonino. I'm just going to cut to the chase. We were able to remove the bullet, which is great. The bad part is that it moved around inside his body causing more problems. He slipped into a coma, which can be a good thing and also bad. Good; because he can heal without going through the pain physically. Bad; because we don't have an exact time of how long he would be in it. The police will soon be up here, and you can inform them on everything that you know."

"I ain't talking to no fucking police!" Black screamed. Before this conversation could get any worse, I asked the doctor could we go see Nino. He informed us that he just got out of surgery and it wouldn't be a good time. Black was upset, but he understood, considering the trauma Nino was in.

Black

Looking at Sophia, I couldn't help but to feel like she was hiding something from me. The way she nervously sat in the passenger seat of my car, biting on her nails, messing with her hair every few seconds. Something in my gut was telling me that is was more to the story. Melody cried silently, sniffing every few seconds in the back seat. "So, what's going to happen here...right now... you are going to tell me everything about that nigga." Sophia looked at me shockingly, then looked towards the back at Melody, as if she could help her.

"What nigga?" she surprisingly asked. Grabbing onto her thigh, I firmly squeezed it to let her know I wasn't playing any fucking games! "Melody please..." she begged. Melody dropped her head on her lap wailing louder.

"It's because of me Black," she cried for like the fourth time tonight. Stopping the car on the side of the road unexpectedly, everyone bodies jerked to the left from the pressure. I didn't have to ask no questions because my facial expressions showed I needed answers. My right fucking hand is in a fucking coma fighting for his life and my sister was blaming it all on her? *What the fuck is going on?* Lifting her head back up, Sophia began to speak.

"Please just hear me out before you judge me. It all started out as a meaningless friendship between me and him. Somebody that could occupy my time because Drew was never around and I was lonely. I never knew it would get this far. Don changed--"

"Don?!" I screamed out.

"Do not judge me! I didn't know... I didn't know that he would shoot him. We started to spend more and more time with one another. I got caught up thinking the grass was greener on the other side. Then he started hanging out with Drew and things spiraled out of control. I swear I didn't mean for any of this to happen, you got to believe me Black. I lost everything! Drew, my dignity, EVERYTHING! If I could rewind back time I swear I would in a heartbeat. You sent Nino to come get me from the bar because now I am sure Drew told you about me seeing someone else and I'm sorry for lashing out on you Sophia. I wouldn't leave with him, so I thought he left. Once I got outside, Don popped up threaten me with a gun. Nino thought he was bluffing and I did too, but we were wrong. He shot him... he shot him with no regret. It's all because of me, I fucked up!"

Listening to everything Melody was telling me, I was appalled. That niggas sat with us at their home, at clubs, all awhile messing with Melody behind Drews back. Sheisty. Melody too. "Yo where he lives and what's his real name?" I asked Sophia starting back up the car.

"I don't know anything about him!" she screamed out in frustration.

"How the fuck you don't know anything about your cousin?"

"Because he is not my cousin! Melody lied! She only said it because Drew caught him in the house the day of the party Melody threw me!"

"Oh, so yall just a bunch of liars? This is what the fuck yall do? Yo, before I say something I might regret, just go in the crib. I'll find out what I want to do with you later," I said to Sophia looking straight in her eyes.

"And what is that supposed to mean Quintel?"

"Close my door."

Watching them walk inside the house, I zoomed away, thinking about my next move. *Fuck the cops trying to find who shot Nino, I knew who did it and needed to handle it first before they did.*

Sophia

I knew it, I knew it, I knew it!

 I knew all of this was going to blow up in my face, I knew it was going to get out of control, but what can I tell a grown woman that was capable of her own decisions? Walking into my apartment, that I wasn't sure I was still considered a resident at, Melody went into the bathroom and turned on the shower. Everything was so tensed in the car, I forgot she was drenched with Nino's blood on her clothing. Going inside of my bedroom I laid on the bed exhausted. *I could've stayed away for all of this.* Taking off my clothes, I got under the sheets hoping to fall asleep quickly.

1:00 AM

Jumping up out of my sleep, a slam from the front door frightened me. Getting out of the bed, I ran to the living room to see Melody lying on the couch staring at the ceiling. "Who was that?" I asked her.

"Black," she responded with no emotions.

"Black? Why did he leave?" I asked rushing to the window, but his car was gone.

"He said he had shit to handle," she responded, still emotionless.

"Why didn't he come and say anything to me? What did he say to you?"

"He came over here to ask about Don. I don't know why he didn't come and wake you up. Maybe you should ask him. I don't know anything anymore," she responded turning her back to face me. I knew she felt like shit. I wouldn't blame her because who knew Don was going to go crazy and shoot Nino? The damage was already done.

"Did you speak to Drew?" I asked her, sitting down on the couch where her feet were.

"No. He doesn't want anything to do with me. That could've been me shot in the hospital and he probably wouldn't have even cared." She paused for a moment before turning back around to look at me. "Soph, do you think that I damaged goods? Would anybody ever want me again?" she cried.

"What? Why would you say that? None of this, as of now is your fault; this was out of your control."

"Don. he said that," she mumbled.

"Don? Fuck him Melody! He was a clown to begin with and I wished you would've noticed. You fucked up! Granted! But, don't you ever think that about yourself. In due time, it will get better. I promise you," I told her moving closer to hug her as we both cried on each other's shoulders.

Waking up the next morning, I called out of work. There was no way I could focus with everything that was parading around in my mind. Melody told me she was going to her mother's house before she left. Just yesterday, my life was everything I imagined and more. That one phone call spiraled everything out of control. Calling Black over and over again, my calls went unanswered. I knew Sophia needed time to herself, so I decided to hit up Shay to see what she was doing, but she responded telling me it was family day. I was officially feeling alone at this point.

Melody

I told Sophia I was going to my mother's house, but I wasn't. I was going to the home that I use to share with the man that I love. I just needed him to hold me, to tell me everything was going to be okay. Pulling up to the front, I took in a deep breathe. Hoping and praying Drew can let his love for me out power my infidelity. Putting my key into the door, the house looked completely the same, nothing was out of place.

"Drew!" I yelled.

I knew he was here because I saw his car parked out front. Walking up the stairs to our bedroom I opened the door, still he wasn't there. "Drew!" I called out again. *Maybe he really did leave*, I sadly thought. Going into the walk in closet, I heard the shower running. *Oh he's in the shower.* Reaching the bathroom door, before I could turn the knob, I heard what sounded like a moan from behind the door. Busting in the bathroom, the moaning increased. I saw a set of two pair of hands pressed against the shower doors. Shocked. Confused. The steam from the hot shower fogged up the doors but I knew it was Drew, I knew his moans from a mile away. He grunted out in pleasure, while whoever he was grinding into was moaning out that she loved him. *Loved him?* Yes, I knew I deserved this, but how did he move on so fast? I couldn't believe this! I wanted to confront him but I would die if I saw him inside of someone else. Walking out of the bathroom, I went and sat on *our* bed, waiting patiently for them to realize they had company.

In deep thought, trying to ignore the moans that escaped under the bathroom door, my phone startled me.

UNKNOWN NUMBER: *Yo?*

ME: *Who is this?*

UNKNOWN NUMBER: *Who the fuck else would be texting you? What I did wasn't enough? You want somebody else's blood on your hands?*

Looking around, I feared I was being watched. An uneasiness took over my body.

UNKNOWN NUMBER: *So now you not going to text back? Yeah, it's me. It's Daddy. Yo come meet me? I'm going to be at my house waiting on you before I go and lay low for a minute. Hurry your ass up too! I can't be here for too long.*

Before I could text back, I heard the shower turn off. Following the sound of laughter... happiness... The door opened and there stood Drew, with a towel wrapped around his toned waist. Before I could say anything, a woman appeared from behind him who seemed to be.....

"What are you doing here?" he had the nerve to ask me.

"What am I doing here? I live here! When the hell were you going to tell me--"

Cutting me off, "None of that matters. What's done is done. We both went our separate ways. That's what you wanted right?" he asked.

"Is this her?" the female asked.

Ignoring her, I turned my attention back to Drew. "You're having a baby Drew?" I yelled.

"Yeah, I'm having a baby," he responded.

"She looks to be about five months Drew! We were together five months ago!" I yelled getting in his face.

"So tell me, five months ago you wasn't fucking that nigga? All those nights you went missing. Me looking for you at your mom's house. Me! Trying to chase you down and shit. You don't think I knew in the back of my mind you weren't out doing you? That phone call just confirmed what I already knew! Yeah, I slipped up one night... Fuck it, now that it's out in the open, I slipped up a few nights. I tried to make it right and make you my wife. But, you rather had fucked the nigga you were fucking. You don't think I knew the pussy felt different? I was fucking you for years ma. This... what me and you had? It's over. You moved on right? This wasn't what you wanted right?"

Stuck. I couldn't explain the feeling I felt. The pain inside of my heart. The tears rushed down my face. I had nothing to say. He was right. I saw the emotions inside of his eyes, I knew he wouldn't had ever wanted me to see what I was seeing right now. The emotions inside of his eyes said one story, but the words that escaped from his mouth said another. With nothing else to say, nothing more to do. I walked away and out of the home I once shared with Drew. Getting inside my car, I wiped the tears that streamed down my face with no control. With only one destination running through my mind to go to, I started the car and drove away without any regret.

Sophia

Rushing inside of my apartment, I dropped my bags and ran into the bathroom. I hated using the bathroom at work because even my coworkers were nasty. I've been calling Melody all day and got no answer. I knew she needed time to herself, but I just wanted to check on her. After using the bathroom, I took off my scrubs to hop into the shower and clean that hospital smell off of me. I still didn't speak to Black also. I never expected him to treat me the way he was doing but deep down I knew I had to be understanding because he was mourning his friend so I couldn't take his actions personal.

After getting out of the shower, the same time I opened the bathroom door was the same time the front door opened and in walked Black. Usually the one to always look on point, he looked stressed. It's only been two days for me, but you could tell it was forty-eight long hours for him. "We need to talk," was all he said before sitting on the couch. Sitting next to him, I waited for him to speak up.

"I don't think I could do this anymore."

"What?" I asked confused.

"Me and you," he responded.

"Black, really?"

"Maybe in the future, but right now. I just need some time."

"Time? Why because of one little lie?"

"One little lie? That's all it is to you right? My right hand man is laid up in the hospital over one *little lie*. That one *little lie* fucked up a lot of shit right now! That one *little lie* could turn into multiple fucking *lies*! You lied for how fucking long? How many months? You had niggas looking like a fool lounging with the nigga and shit. I don't even know what the fuck else you could've possibly lied about! Who knows who else he would have hurt. You see where that one *little lie* got you? How do I know I could trust you?"

"Black you're honestly blaming the wrong person! It's not my fault! I was just trying to be a friend to Melody!"

"That's right and you succeed." Getting up Black went towards the door with me heavy on his toes.

"So what does this mean? It's over?" I asked him.

"I just need time to think. I can't fuck with liars."

"Black you're being dramatic!"

"Dramatic? Tell that shit to Nino fighting for his life in that hospital bed. I'm out. Ima holla at you later," Black said reaching for the knob. The whole time he couldn't even look me in the eyes to announce our little 'break'. He knew what he just said was a low blow and I didn't mean it that way. I knew this wasn't about me and him right now, more of his emotions so I let him walk away for the time being.

ME: *Just know that I love you, and I'm sorry.*

After texting Black, I put my phone on the centerpiece, I grabbed the remote and turned on the television.

"That was so tragic, the flames spread wildly in seconds. It wasn't anything anyone could do. I saw him around from time to time. He was a young man who stayed to himself. I will be praying for his family and the lady who was found." A middle age woman spoke in the reporter's microphone.

"Donovan Smith was one of the victims that were trapped inside his home when it started to surround with flames. When firefighters approached the scene, it wasn't anything they could do. The blaze was so strong it took over thirty minutes for them to put it out. This was just a sad tragic, tragic story that took place last night," the reporter spoke into the mic. Suddenly, a picture of Don flashed across the screen. *What?* "As for the female that was found in the home also, she's currently still unidentified and we are working our hardest to find out who she is. We reportedly heard of a female that he spends a lot of time with, but currently have no name. This is Sasha Rogers reporting live from News six."

Is that the reason why Melody didn't answer the phone? Phlegm build up in my throat. Rushing to the bathroom I threw up everything I ate today. *It can't be.*

CPSIA information can be obtained
at www.ICGtesting.com
Printed in the USA
LVHW041627130919
631009LV00009B/362